Let There Be Laughter

A TREASURY OF GREAT JEWISH HUMOR & WHAT IT ALL MEANS

Let There Be Laughter

Michael Krasny

WILLIAM MORROW
An Imprint of HarperCollins*Publishers*

HarperCollins books may be purchased for educational, business, or sales promotional use. For information, please email the Special Markets Department at SPsales@harpercollins.com.

FIRST EDITION

Designed by Bonni Leon-Berman

Library of Congress Cataloging-in-Publication Data has been applied for.

ISBN 978-0-06-242204-0

16 17 18 19 20   RRD   10 9 8 7 6 5 4 3

TO MY PARENTS,

MY WIFE & CHILDREN &

MY SISTER & BROTHER—

WHO ALL HAVE

LOVED & CHERISHED

JEWISH HUMOR.

CONTENTS

Let There Be Laughter

Introduction

STEVE ALLEN, the first television talk-show host and a non-Jew, once troubled himself with the task of assessing the percentage of Jews involved in the American world of comedy—whether in performing or writing and producing—and he came up with a figure exceeding 80 percent. It may not necessarily have been quite that high at the time, and perhaps isn't now, but from vaudeville and the Catskills to stand-up comedy, television and film comedy writing, and such popular culture phenomena as *Mad* and *Cracked* magazines, the *National Lampoon,* and the *Borowitz Report,* Jews have continued to play overwhelmingly dominant roles in the world of comedy and humor—even Jews short on much if any sense of Yiddishkeit, Judaism, or what might be termed a Jewish sensibility.

How do we account for such dominance? Gene pool? Culture? A business that a people found themselves at ease working in, through generations, like the Chinese with laundries, the Vietnamese with nail salons, Italians with pizzerias, Koreans with grocery stores, or the Irish with pubs? Or, for that matter, Jews with delis or Jews in the garment industry or Jews as doctors? It is a challenging question and one with no simple answers. But consider the wild range and diversity of the major figures from the world of Jewish humor, through the generations, from the vaudeville and Borscht Belt performers like George Jessel and Fanny Brice; the zaniness of the Marx Brothers; the early goofball comedy of Sid Caesar and Jerry Lewis; the cleverness of the married team of George Burns and Gracie Allen; the breakthrough humor of Shelley Berman and Buddy Hackett; the amiable silliness of Milton ("Welcome, Ladies and Germs") Berle; the inimitable wit of Jack Benny ("Give me golf clubs, fresh air, and a beautiful partner and you can keep the golf clubs and the fresh air"); the brilliant parody lyrics of Tom Lehrer—

Oh, the Protestants hate the Catholics,
And the Catholics hate the Protestants,
And the Hindus hate the Moslems,
And everybody hates the Jews

—the slapstick and silliness of the Three Stooges ("And what were you doing in Paris?" "Oh, looking over the Paris sites"); the pop-song satire of Allan Sherman ("Oh, Harry Lewis perished in the service of his Lord/He was trampling through the warehouse where the drapes of Roth are stored"); the mordant satire of Mort Sahl ("A family of agnostics moves into a neighborhood and a question mark is burned on their lawn"); the comic genius and zaniness of Danny Kaye, Phil Silvers, Red Buttons, Jack Carter, Victor Borge, Irwin Corey, and Peter Sellers; the nightclub shtick of Shecky Greene; the aggressive and mocking, caustic humor of Lenny Bruce, Jack E. Leonard or Don Rickles, Joan Rivers and Andrew Dice Clay; the sweet, schmaltzy nostalgia humor of Sam Levinson, Myron Cohen, or Harry Golden; the delightful comedies of Neil Simon; the brilliant wit of writers such as S. J. Perelman, Joseph Heller, Philip Roth, Stanley Elkin, and Mordecai Richler; the comedy column writing of Art Buchwald and Calvin Trillin; or the comedic filmmaking of Billy Wilder, Sacha Baron Cohen, Ivan Reitman, Nora Ephron, Harold Ramis, the Coen brothers, the Zucker brothers and Jim Abrahams; Judd Apatow, Adam Sandler, and Seth Rogen.

Where do contemporary figures such as Roseanne Barr, Jerry Seinfeld, Jon Stewart, and Billy Crystal, or for that matter, Mel Brooks, Woody Allen, Albert Brooks, Richard Lewis, Gilda Radner, Gary Shandling, Larry David, David Brenner, Howard Stern, Richard Belzer, David Steinberg, Robert Klein, Sarah Silverman, Lewis Black, Chelsea Handler, and Amy Schumer all fit in? Do they? Are there, aside from Jewishness, any real connections or links in all of the wild diversity of the generations? Is there a tribal gestalt of Jewish humor? A lineage? A religious or cultural taproot?

No matter. The contributions of generations of Jews in comedy is something I cannot possibly overstate. On the other hand, notwithstanding towering iconic figures like Hank Greenberg, Sandy Koufax, and Mark Spitz, another question lingers. What is the shortest book ever written? Answer: *Great Jewish Sports Heroes.*

I believe the first time I told a Jewish joke was in the tenth grade. My social studies teacher, a curmudgeon, was talking to us about the Middle East. I remembered a joke that I thought might amuse sour-faced old Mr. Lehman. So, after class, I asked him if he knew what the fastest thing on water was. He bit and I delivered the punch line: "A Jew in a canoe on the Suez Canal." It brought him to laughter so hard he had to hold on to his desk.

Fast-forward over four decades later when (name-drop alert) the film director Barry Levinson introduced me to Dustin Hoffman as an English professor and public radio talk-show host who knew more Jewish jokes than anyone else. I could hardly confirm that description, but in the years since telling the Suez Canal joke, I collected an extensive bounty of Jewish jokes. And I relished telling them to Jews and non-Jews alike.

But I was not cut out to be a comedian.

I wanted to be a novelist.

I even got a Ph.D in literature, thinking that, in addition to deferring conscription to Vietnam jungles, it would help me realize my novelist dream. I became a scholar and then, with an unexpected detour, I embarked on a career as a talk-show host on public radio, known more for handling serious and newsworthy subject matter than for Jewish joke telling.

Yet my interest in Jewish jokes increased. I began to do routines of Jewish joke telling at small and then larger venues. As I became more widely known as a radio host, with one of the nation's largest locally produced public radio listening audiences, the demand increased for me to mount the stage and tell Jewish jokes. I was also able to interview, throughout my years in broadcasting, a number of the great Jewish comedians. But I was not just telling Jewish jokes. I was also analyzing them.

The initial spur to explain meaning in Jewish jokes came from my reading Freud's *Jokes and Their Relation to the Unconscious*, a book that tells us how jokes discharge aggression and anxiety, and, of course, conceal deep and often repressed sexual meaning. As a teacher of literature, I came to view jokes, like fiction, as portals to knowledge and ways to see how the powers of storytelling and laughter are linked.

I decided to write a book on the great Jewish jokes and what they mean.

This was a formidable task. Why? Because jokes are often more successfully told than read. The Internet has made many good Jewish jokes simply a click away, and a number of Jewish joke books were already out in the world. But I had a wide-ranging repertoire and I wanted to focus on meaning.

Once I started working on the task I'd set for myself, I expanded into a broad discussion of Jewish humor by bringing in folkloric and stand-up material, television, film, cartoons and comics, as well as jokes. I also realized that I had a wonderful set of anecdotes from personal experience, including decades of interviewing many famous and illustrious people. I wasn't writing a novel. But I was, in both the jokes and stories, creating narrative.

There is a joke about an Esperanto convention, Esperanto being the once highly touted universal language. In the joke, everyone at the Esperanto convention is speaking Yiddish.

Today, Jewish or non-Jewish, most people need a search engine to learn what the majority of Yiddish words mean.

Jewish jokes mourn loss, especially of the Yiddish language and culture, both having endured secular change and assimilation. But many jokes succeed in creating humor out of these and other losses, the most powerful of all possibly being loss of religious belief, piety, ritual, and identity. Jewish humor highlights suffering and neurosis but also emerges with laughter. Much Jewish humor simply celebrates life.

So-called Jewish American princess jokes are often misogynistic, even anti-Semitic, but they also celebrate Jewish material success.

Jews are portrayed in jokes as being overly greedy schmucks and also as poor schlemiels.

Jewish jokes canonize Jewish mothers and Jewish grandmothers but also display despair, impotence, and even rage about their overprotectiveness and guilt making.

Sex and marriage are celebrated in Jewish jokes and are also mercilessly ridiculed. Jewish jokes reveal profound feelings of chauvinism and chosenness as well as deep feelings of inferiority and self-laceration.

If ambivalence is the emotional currency of Jewish lives, then the humor of Jews embodies and even embraces it. Perhaps that explains why Jewish humor has become, in many respects, inseparable from American humor. Or even, in our global age, universal humor. A lot of Jewish jokes cross over to other nationalities and cultures and are indeed universal. But, paradoxically, many stand utterly alone and nearly cry out repeatedly with three simple words: WE ARE DIFFERENT.

Jewish Mothers & Jewish Bubbies

A Jewish grandmother takes her handsome young grandson to the beach. The boy is close to the incoming waves and unexpectedly gets knocked down by a powerful one and is washed out into the ocean. The Jewish grandmother, unable to swim, screams in terror that her grandchild is drowning, pleads for someone to save him, and prays to God for help. As if God hears her anguished cries, a young muscular lifeguard appears and dives into the water. She, meanwhile, is still distraught, terrified that the child has been under the water too long to survive. The lifeguard brings the blue-looking little boy to shore and begins to administer mouth-to-mouth resuscitation on him while the grandmother continues to pray. Soon water spurts from the boy's mouth and he is breathing. The lifeguard reassures the grandmother that her grandson is going to be okay. Whereupon the old lady nods, unclasps her hands from the prayer position, and says to the lifeguard, with a bit of an edge in her voice, "HE HAD A HAT."

An older Jewish woman, Mrs. Rosenblum, signs up for a difficult trek up the Himalayas with a mostly youthful and vigorous Sierra Club—type group who are told, when they complete the journey to the top, they will meet a guru. With an effort that astonishes and amazes all members of the group and, especially, its youthful leader, she manages to make it to the top. Once they're all there, the leader tells the group that the guru lives in a cave, which he points to and says, "Right there at the top of the Himalayas." The young leader informs them: "The guru receives visitors, but please be advised that you can only say three words to him. This is an extraordinary opportunity to be in the presence of, as well as speak any three words of your choice to, this most revered and venerated guru."

Each of the intrepid hikers files in to meet the guru and speak whatever three words they wish to utter in his presence. This includes Mrs. Rosenblum. When she emerges from the cave, the young leader asks her if she saw the guru. "Yes," she replies. "I saw him." The young leader then asks, "And did you say three words to him?" Mrs. Rosenblum replies, "Yes. I said three words." The curious young leader then asks, "May I ask what those words were?" Mrs. Rosenblum answers: "SHELDON, COME HOME."

J

EWISH MOTHERS are quite possibly seen as the most overbearing and overly protective mothers of them all, and have yet to be eclipsed in popular culture by either the tiger mom or the helicopter mother. Philip Roth's Sophie Portnoy, in his nationally best-selling novel *Portnoy's Complaint,* led the archetypal way as the mother of all Jewish mothers—as unrivaled in her ability to tear down her son, Alexander, as she was in revering him. We had Dan Greenberg's *How to Be a Jewish Mother* and Bruce J. Friedman's *A Mother's Kisses.* There have been a host of other books, films, and TV shows that served to provide a well-established picture of the Jewish mother being unlike any other mother in the guilt-dispensing category or in smothering overprotectiveness . . . or in adoration.

My own mother would nag and scold as much as kiss. Unfailingly, she would also sob whenever she put the recording on our small Victrola of Connie Francis singing "My Yiddishe Momme." Her mother, my bubbie, was extremely different from her—not only rooted in the Old World of Russia, but also much easier and simpler to deal with (until senility set in). She was less prone to nag and scold and gave fewer (though wetter) kisses. Perhaps, as the old saw has it, grandparents have greater ease with their grandchildren than parents because they don't have to raise them. Yet bubbies like mine, with Old World roots, could be even more overly protective than their sons or daughters. A woman friend of mine told me once that when she stayed overnight at her grandmother's house, she was not allowed to go out to pick up the morning paper in the driveway without her bubbie walking with her and holding her hand. This was as true when she was eighteen as it had been when she was eight.

Another woman friend of mine, the songwriter Rita Abrams, told me when she was in her twenties, her aging grandmother took her to the movies. As they entered the theater, her grand-mother commanded, "Get yourself some POPCORN!" Rita said, "It's okay, bubbie, I don't want any popcorn." Her bubbie repeated, "Get yourself some POPCORN!" Rita again de-clined. But when her bubbie once more insisted, she gave in and got the popcorn. After the movie, they went to dinner.

Looking at Rita's plate, her grandmother observed, "You haven't eaten very much." Rita said, "I'm not very hungry." Her grandmother scolded, "Of COURSE you're not hungry—after all that popcorn!"

Rita's story about her bubbie is reminiscent of the joke about the Jewish mother who brings over two new ties as a birthday gift for her adult son. Later, in the evening, the two meet for dinner and the son is wearing one of the ties. His mother takes one look at him and says, "You didn't like the other tie?"

Mothers and grandmothers can often be seen through a nearly identical lens. The bubbie, however, is a special embodiment of Jewish motherhood—but one that can probably be more accurately described as a Jewish mother on steroids. Bubbies can be pictured as being even more consumed with pride and love for their children's children than for their own.

Why have Jewish mothers and grandmothers been fodder now for years for such a wide range of jokes that nearly sanctify their over-the-top feelings of love and pride in their children? The definition of a Jewish genius? An ordinary boy with a Jewish mother. Or Jesus obviously being a Jewish boy because he thought his mother was a virgin and his mother thought he was God. Jewish mothers, especially, are often portrayed as braggarts about their children at the same time that they are ridiculed for creating neuroses in them, as in the one about the

Jewish mother who boasts to all of her friends that her son sees a psychoanalyst six times a week and, she adds proudly, "He talks mainly about me." Or the Jewish mother who says, "Yes, my son is in a wheelchair and yes, he can walk perfectly well. But thank God he doesn't have to!" Are these the same Jewish mothers who are compared in jokes to Rottweilers or, worse yet, vultures (the difference is vultures wait until you are dead to eat your heart out).

Yet generations pass and time and assimilation march on. Many of the young Jewish women thought to be prototypes for portrayals in Jewish American princess jokes are now grandmothers and even great-grandmothers. However, distinctive typing of Jewish mothers and grandmothers remains alive in many of the jokes we tell, hear, and read. We can even go to the line, from an unknown source, about what the mother of Christopher Columbus might have said if she were a Jewish mother (and there are scholars who claim Columbus was a Jew!): "I don't care what you discovered. You didn't call. You didn't write."

The joke ending with "Sheldon, come home" has another version to it in which the Jewish mother says, "Enough is enough." For me, the first version strikes a stronger chord. I told the joke with that ending to my friend the actor Peter Coyote, who, though born Jewish (née Cohon), had by that time become an ordained Zen priest. I kidded him that the joke was obviously about men like him. I also told it to Ram Dass because it easily could have been about him as well, a Jewish boy who went to Harvard and became a spiritual teacher with a name change from Richard Alpert plucked right out of the East (and I don't mean Brooklyn). The joke resonates with present-day Jews by virtue of the fact that many have taken up Eastern, especially Buddhist, practices. The signifiers that denote this phenomenon, Bagel Buddhist and JewBu, have become part of the popular lexicon. I know a young woman whose mother insisted she go on JDate to find a Jewish mate. She did and soon began to write back and forth with a young Jewish man who seemed promising to her, until he asked her if she practiced yoga. When she responded that she was more into cardio, he sent back a message, completely in caps, that read: I CANNOT DATE ANYONE WHO IS NOT A YOGINI BECAUSE YOU CAN'T BE ZEN.

The name Sheldon dates that joke to another era—few Jewish mothers name their sons Sheldon anymore. It's a name that has nearly disappeared, like Irving. (My parents knew a man, born Irving Irving, who legally changed his name to Irwin Irwin). But the joke really, at its core, is about a Jewish mother willing to climb the highest mountain peak and do whatever she needs to do to tell her son to come home. She speaks for all the Jewish mothers who wish their sons (and daughters) would come back to their religious home, Judaism. In that sense, the joke is reminiscent of the old ditty I heard as a kid in Cleveland, which juxtaposes the passivity of the old world of the European shtetl with a more assimilated, aggressive America where Jewish boys in Jewish fraternities like ZBT dated shiksas (Gentile girls) on the holiest of nights. A Jewish mother's lament:

Ai yi yi. Zeta Beta Tau. What have they done to my little Yiddish boy?
I sent my son to college to learn to read and write and now he's dating shiksas on Yom Kippur night.

The Himalaya-climbing Jewish mother's motivation for so arduous a trek, however, is also to scold her son, to heap guilt on him for leaving his faith, yes, but likely even more for leaving her! This, like the joke about the grandmother complaining about a lost hat after her grandson has nearly drowned, is essentially all about a satirized image of maternal "Jewish" traits.

Two Jewish mothers see each other walking down a street. The first gives the second an effusive mazel tov on the engagement of her daughter. "How did you know my daughter was engaged?" the second woman asks the first, who says, "I read the announcement in the paper. And she's marrying a doctor!" "Yes," the proud mother says. The other woman goes on, "And wasn't this the same daughter who was married once before to a lawyer?" "Yes," says the mother of the bride-to-be. "You have a good memory. That marriage, unfortunately, didn't work out." The first woman adds, "And this is the same daughter who was married to an accountant, no?" "Yes. You're right again," says the mother, sighing and adding, "That, too, didn't work out." Whereupon the first woman enthuses, "From one daughter such *naches!*"

The joke begins with celebration and ends with the Yiddish word *naches*, a word used to describe the joy and pride a parent derives from a child's accomplishments—apparently in this case, at least to the well-wisher, one unmarred by divorces. Embedded in that Yiddish word is a whole panoply of Jewish cultural values unto the generations. *Naches* is central to bubbies, too, of course, in the line about the Jewish grandmother who says to another Jewish woman of her vintage, "So if you didn't want me to show you photos of my grandchildren, why did you say hello to me?" My brother Victor reported to me that he saw a Jewish grandmother carrying an enormous purse with large-sized photos of her grandchildren pasted on the outside. Curious as to what she might have been hauling in the large handbag, he asked her. Her quick response: "Nothing. I carry it so everyone can see my grandkids."

Naches often goes back to accomplishments. Jewish mothers or grandmothers can be masterful at mentioning a son or daughter or grandson or granddaughter's achievements—especially if they are academic ("He happens not only to have graduated with honors, but is also in a special club called Phi Beta Kappa!") or professional ("She just finished her residency. I can't remember the specialty, though I know it's a very very important one"). *Naches* comes, of course, in many forms and varieties, including who (or what, as in career or vocation) a child or grandchild marries. When Michael Dukakis, the former governor of Massachusetts, ran against George W. Bush and Jews found out his wife, Kitty, was Jewish, they spoke about "*naches* from Dukakis." The highest form of *naches* for a Jewish American mother or grandmother, obviously, would be to have a child grow up to be the first Jewish leader of the free world.

A Jewish mother is sitting at her daughter's inauguration as the nation's first Jewish president. At the inauguration, a stranger leans over and whispers in the mother's ear, "You must be so proud. Your daughter is the president of the United States!" Whereupon the Jewish mother responds, "Yes. But her brother is a doctor!"

For a daughter to marry a doctor was, for many years, for many Jews, the highest form of *naches* short of having a son who managed to become one. Just as there often appears to me to be a greater number than there used to be of Jewish alcoholics—recall the old adage "the shicker is the goy," meaning "the drunk is the non-Jew"), there has also been a decrease in the number of Jewish doctors. Is this loss of Jewish identity? Assimilation? *Lower physician pay?*

If you ask the question at what stage a fetus becomes viable for Jews, you still hear the answer "after med school." Yet the novelist Amy Tan told me she heard the same joke told about Chinese Americans. You could also probably, in today's world, update the *naches* joke to a Jewish woman congratulating another on the engagement of her son to a doctor of the same sex.

Jackie Mason delivered a line about how Jewish male children were hounded by their mothers to become doctors; and, if they couldn't become doctors, they could, according to Mason, at least become lawyers; and if they couldn't become doctors or lawyers and were, in his word "retarded," they could become accountants.

Could Jackie Mason get away without giving offense with a word like "retarded" in today's politically-sensitive-to-language world? Racial jokes also fall into that category.

The great short story writer Grace Paley, a proud Jewish mother, spoke glowingly to me of having a black grandchild. She, like many Jewish mothers of her generation and beyond, who were political activists and strongly sympathetic to civil rights issues, got *naches* from children they brought up as nonbigoted and progressive, who married someone black. By contrast, there were other Jewish mothers who went into a how-can-you-do-this-to-me-or-us howling response. This joke is all too revealing of an attitude among some urban and suburban Jews (and whites in general) of the pre—and even post—*Guess Who's Coming to Dinner* era, a film in which a young daughter brings home the man she has fallen in love with, a black doctor, played by Sidney Poitier.

A husband of a different religion was all too often seen by

Jews as being bad for the Jews and, until recent years, even a *shanda* (a shame or a scandal), especially among the more religious. When a Jewish guy in my Cleveland neighborhood, where I grew up, married out of the faith, his parents sat shiva and mourned him as dead. My mother told me of another Jewish mother who snuck into the church to see her son bowing down with his bride at the altar before the priest who was marrying them. My Yiddishe momme solemnly told me how that Jewish mother died on the spot from a heart attack, a tale she had heard from other Jewish mothers. Of course, years later, I found this story to be untrue, since the mother had simply moved away to another neighborhood and was still very much alive.

A boy's mother takes him to his first day of school and reassuringly says, before dropping him off, "Please, bubbeleh, have a wonderful day at school. Enjoy! And, bubbeleh, please be sure to eat all of the lunch I packed for you. I'll be waiting to pick you up as soon as school is over. I love you, bubbeleh!" When school is out, the mother is there. She kisses her son and eagerly asks, "How was school, bubbeleh?" "Fine," the boy answers. "And what did you learn in school, bubbeleh?" The boy answers, "I learned my name is not bubbeleh."

The meaning behind the obvious humor of a boy knowing himself only as *"bubbeleh"* speaks volumes. That Yiddish word is derived from "bubbe," the word for grandmother. Like *mameleh*, the word my father called his first granddaughter, my niece Sheryl (named for her grandmother Sarah), *bubbeleh* is a word of tenderness and adoration. It is a word redolent of *naches* and it unites generations etymologically and across genders. I have an odd stray memory of the singer Neil Diamond calling Henry Winkler (the Fonz in *Happy Days*) *bubbeleh*. I have another of a Jewish friend proudly announcing to his young son, while the two were watching *Happy Days*, that "the Fonz is Jewish." That *naches* derived from the fact that there exists association with fellow Jews that can actually go nearly as far as maternal *naches*. Adam Sandler built a number of versions of his famous Hanukkah song around it. But *naches* and its connection to loving Jewish mothers and grandmothers is but one side of the equation. Jewish mothers, especially, are often portrayed in Jewish jokes as overly critical, impossibly demanding nags who are the bane of their children's lives.

Before I get to that other side—a side that has produced much material for jokes, parody, satire, cartoons, and all vari-

eties of hyperbole—I want to relate a true Jewish mother story
my older daughter told me. The story is about a friend of hers,
let's call her Amy, who met a stylish, older Jewish woman at
a luncheon. After starting a conversation with Amy, the older
Jewish woman determined that Amy was single and the same
age as her son. She began to rhapsodize about her son. How
charming and intelligent and charismatic and accomplished
he was! But, above all, how incredibly handsome. "A twin to
JFK Jr.," she insisted. She went on: "In fact, you would not
believe how much those two look alike. Like identical twins.
You couldn't possibly tell them apart. When I saw the photos
of JKF Jr. after he died I nearly fainted. My son looks just like
him. I warn him against, God forbid, becoming a narcissist.
But not to worry. He is kindhearted. Tall, dark, handsome, and
kindhearted. Can you do any better than that?"

So the two are fixed up. Amy is excited. She goes to the
door expecting to see a JFK Jr. doppelgänger, a living incarna-
tion or replication of the scion of our thirty-fifth president and
Jackie O. "Instead," she tells my daughter, "he was the size of
a jockey. With a sunken, caved-in chest, acne, and a nose that
nearly took over his face."

When I heard this story from her, my daughter asked
me, "How could this mother have been so blind, Dad? Do

you really think she believed her son looked like JFK Jr.'s twin?"

"Well," I said. "She *is* a Jewish mother."

The other side of the equation is with the Jewish mothers and grandmothers who are often portrayed, even those with free-flowing love and *naches,* as putting enormous and guilt-heavy demands on their children and grandchildren, smothering them, and even being relentless and ruthless. The object of a lot of that kind of behavior, much Jewish humor reveals, is (drumbeat) *naches*! The maternal desire for *naches* can be tied to incessant disapproval of nearly everything, including mate choices.

A young Jewish man is in a synagogue at a Friday-night service. The rabbi cannot help but notice from the pulpit that the young man looks sad and unhappy. When the service ends, the rabbi goes to him. "You look so sad," the compassionate rabbi says. "What's eating you?" The man frowns and proceeds to tell the rabbi how he has been romantically involved with a number of women, how he took each home to meet his mother, and how she disliked every one of them. The rabbi has a suggestion. With the Internet the young man can find someone who has interests in common with his mother. Couldn't that make a difference? The young man is grateful and promises to follow the rabbi's advice. When he appears at services weeks later, the rabbi notices a countenance on him even more doleful. The rabbi goes over to him after the service ends and asks, "What happened? I thought you were going to follow my advice?" "I did," says the young man. "I found a woman who not only had interests like my mother. She looked like my mother, spoke like her, even cooked like her." The rabbi is puzzled. "So what was the problem?" The young man says: "My father disliked her."

A woman friend of mine, married for decades to her cardiologist husband, tells the tale of being at her in-laws' fiftieth anniversary party. Her husband, her often abrasive mother-in-law, and she were conversing by themselves when, unexpectedly and utterly out of character, her mother-in-law said, "I don't know how she does it, but every year your wife gets better looking." Almost in shock, my woman friend blurted out, "Why, Mom. That's the nicest thing you have ever said to me." At which point her mother-in-law snapped, "I wasn't talking to you!"

A young Jewish man tells his mother he plans on marrying and invites her to meet his chosen bride-to-be. He asks the bride-to-be and two other attractive women friends of hers to stand in a row, and after his mother arrives, he asks her if she can pick out the woman he plans on marrying. Without hesitation, his mother goes right to the bride-to-be and says "Her!" The son is dumbfounded and wants to know how his mother could possibly have selected the right woman so quickly and unerringly. His mother answers: "She's the one I didn't like."

Jewish mothers and Jewish grandmothers are as often portrayed as being as disapproving and difficult as they are overbearing, impossible, martyrlike, and petty. They are seen as insufferable, even though they are also overly loving and protective, with over-the-top *naches* bragging and incomparable mother hennishness.

A Jewish man goes to see his psychiatrist and tells him, right off, that he had a dream the night before that the psychiatrist was his mother. "Okay," the psychiatrist says. "Let's find out what this means. Tell me everything you did from the time you woke up this morning until you came here. Everything!" The Jewish man begins, "Well, let's see. First I got out of bed, then I showered and shaved, combed my hair and got dressed, and went downstairs and had a doughnut." Whereupon the shrink fires back at him, "You call that a breakfast!"

The guilt-heaping Jewish mother can be seen in the now classic comic dialogue between the landmark duo of Elaine May and Mike Nichols. May plays the archetypal Jewish mother and Nichols plays her son Arthur, a rocket scientist. Their phone conversation is built entirely on the mother's haranguing her son for not calling. At the beginning of the skit, the mother says: "It's your mother. Remember me?" and, later, when her son tells her he feels "awful" for not calling her, she says, "If only I could believe that. I'd be the happiest woman in the world." Think of the paradox. A child's guilt for not attending to the need of his Jewish mother equals her supreme happiness.

And speaking of archetypal guilt-inducing mothers, Philip Roth definitely put a premium on them with Alexander Portnoy's mother, Sophie.

Roth's *Portnoy's Complaint* was a shocking novel when it first appeared back in 1969, with all of its emphasis on masturbation and horniness ("Did Roth's character really have sex with a piece of liver?" a Gentile woman friend of mine asked me). A story I enjoy telling, which I told Roth in one of the interviews we did on air, was about the time I went into a local public library with my then teenage daughter to look for books for her to read. There, in a section marked BOOKS FOR TEENS, was *Portnoy's Complaint.*

Portnoy's Complaint gave new meaning to the word "phallocentric," but it also took on the caricature of the Jewish mother in Sophie, who, holding a knife while her son refuses to eat, appeared to be threatening him with literal castration—possibly even murder. This was the same mother who knew no limit in praising her darling.

A long monologue full of shtick, the novel includes Portnoy ranting to his psychiatrist about his Jewish mother telling him that she met another Jewish mother on the street and heard the other Jewish mother brag about her son. This son, with the Yiddish phallic name of Seymour Schmuck, is a world-famous surgeon with an incredible home and gorgeous, brilliant daughters who gives his parents bountiful, inestimable naches.

"Do you remember Seymour Schmuck, Alex?" she asks me, or Aaron Putz or Howard Shlong, or some yo-yo I am supposed to have known in grade school twenty-five years ago, and of whom I have no recollection whatsoever. "Well, I met his mother on the street today, and she told me that Seymour is now the biggest brain surgeon in the entire Western Hemisphere. He owns six different split-level ranch-type houses made all of fieldstone in Livingston, and belongs to the boards of eleven synagogues, all brand new and designed by Marc Kugel, and his two little daughters . . . are so beautiful that they are already under contract to Metro, and so brilliant that they should be in college . . . *And how happy he makes his parents!*" Alex concludes to his shrink, "And you know, the implication is, when are *you* going to get married already. In Newark and the surrounding suburbs this is apparently the question on everybody's lips: WHEN IS ALEXANDER PORTNOY GOING TO STOP BEING SELFISH AND GIVE HIS PARENTS, WHO ARE SUCH WONDERFUL PEOPLE, GRANDCHILDREN?"

Roth does not limit his skewering of Jewish mothers in *Portnoy's Complaint* to the guilt-heaping, *naches*-hungry Sophie. He also has his main character, Alex, tell of a young boy named Ronald Nimkin, a good, obedient Jewish boy who has always been totally compliant with his mother's demands, and who commits suicide. Ronald hangs himself from the shower head. A dutiful boy right to the end, he has a note pinned to his chest that reads: "Mrs. Blumenthal called. Please bring your mahjongg rules to the game tonight."

A poignant scene. A man is on his deathbed with his loving daughter by his side. It is clear he is fading fast and his death is drawing nigh. With his voice weak and barely audible, he suddenly tells his daughter he smells kugel. "Yes," she says. "Mom is making a kugel." Could she, he asks his daughter, get him a piece so, before he dies, he could have a final taste of his wife's delicious kugel? "Of course, Daddy," she says as she bounds over to the kitchen to fulfill her father's dying wish. In the meantime, her father is barely hanging on, and when she returns she sits down again at his bedside and folds her hands but says nothing. Barely able to utter the words, he asks,

"Where's the kugel?" His daughter answers, "Mom says it's for after."

We can substitute the last two words, "for after," in the kugel joke with "for the shiva." The real point of the joke is the Jewish mother being so practical-minded and harsh that she denies her husband's deathbed wish just to taste the kugel she is preparing for the company who will visit and pay their respects after he is gone.

This could easily be categorized as a Jewish-wife joke. But the word "mom" appears in it twice, and as we saw with Sophie Portnoy, food for the traditional Jewish mother can be a matter of life or death. The Yiddish phrase *ess, ess, mayn kind*, meaning "eat, eat, my child," is central to the role of the archetypal Jewish mother who is both nurturing, wanting her child to eat for growth and health, but also commanding, ordering the child to eat lest (God forbid!) growth be stunted or health be affected. As a boy, I would hear Jewish mothers, including my own, talk about their children being "good eaters" or "bad eaters."

Jewish mothers are also portrayed, as the one is in the kugel joke, as being overly concerned with what other people think. There was obvious concern and pride invested in what others might think of these Jewish mothers based on their children's ability to eat. My sister, Lois, now herself a Jewish mother and grandmother, will never be at peace over the fact that our beloved mother sent her to Fresh Air Camp, concerned Lois was too thin. What might others think? That she did not feed her daughter enough? That she was a bad mother?

The fact is, the Jewish-mother stereotype parodied in guilt-themed jokes is now dated, though vestiges and, of course, the jokes all remain.

A Jewish mother's daughter calls to inform her that she has fallen in love with a wonderful man and is getting married. The mother is ecstatic and eager to know all the details. However, before she can inquire about her daughter's fiancé, the daughter informs her that he is [insert ethnicity here]. The daughter then tells her mother that her husband-to-be is unemployed. But, the daughter exclaims, she loves him madly and intends to be his wife. To her surprise, her mother tells her that she and her fiancé are welcome to come and stay as long as they want. "Your father," the mother says, "will sleep on the couch and the two of you can sleep in our bedroom." Whereupon her daughter asks, "But what about you, Mother? Where will you stay?" Her mother answers: "Don't worry about me, darling. As soon as we hang up, I intend to put my head in the oven."

The Jewish mother in the joke prefers martyrdom to living with an interfaith or interracial marriage for her daughter, but it is important to note, given the strong bourgeois values of many Jewish Americans, the Jewish daughter's choice of a mate is also a violation of her mother's wishes that she marry someone with a lucrative job, a man who is a good provider of *naches* if not money. The mother will provide a roof and shelter for her daughter and her daughter's fiancé, but she will give up her own life, imposing a lifetime of guilt on her daughter.

The generational clash in Jewish values is on display in this next joke, where a daughter tries to enlist her mother's help in dating following a failed marriage.

Hi, Mom. Can I leave the kids with you tonight?
You're going out?
Yes.
With whom?
With a friend.

I don't know why you left your husband. He is such a good man.

I didn't leave him. He left me!

You let him leave you, and now you go out with anybodies and nobodies.

I do not go out with anybody. Can I bring over the kids?

I never left you to go out with anybody except your father.

There are lots of things you did and I don't.

What are you hinting at?

Nothing. I just want to know if I can bring the kids over tonight.

You're going to stay the night with him? What will your husband say if he finds out?

My EX-husband. I don't think he would be bothered. From the day he left me, he probably never slept alone!

So you're going to sleep over at this loser's place?

He's not a loser.

A man who goes out with a divorced woman with children is a loser, a parasite.

I don't want to argue. Should I bring over the kids or not?

Poor children, with such a mother.

Such a what?

With no stability. No wonder your husband left you.

ENOUGH!!!

Don't scream at me. You probably scream at this loser, too.

Now you're worried about this loser?

Ah, so you see, he is a loser. I spotted him immediately.
Good-bye, Mother.
Wait! Don't hang up! When are you bringing them over?
I'm not bringing them over! I'm not going out!
If you never go out, how do you expect to meet anyone?

The mother's ambivalence about her daughter's divorced status is maddening—she wants her daughter to be a responsible and devoted wife and mother at the same time that she recognizes the need for her daughter to find someone to replace her no-good, two-timing husband. But also, of course, the Jewish mother is a doting Jewish grandmother. She makes her daughter feel guilty for not being able to keep a husband and provide an intact home for her (the mother's) grandchildren. The power of a Jewish mother to instill guilt in her child is right at the core of this dialogue. Moreover, the Jewish mother can see only clouds in what could be the silver lining of losing a rotten son-in-law.

It may go without saying, but I'll say it: traditional Jewish mothers or Jewish grandmothers want their sons, daughters, and grandchildren wed. My sister, Lois, divorced for many years, was convinced, even when our mother was in a coma, that Mom would come out of it if only Lois could announce that she had found a worthy groom. A Jewish woman friend of mine, in her sixties and a Jewish grandmother herself, confided to me that she drove long distances to shop for groceries lest she run into people she knew in her own neighborhood who might ask her about the marital status of her single, forty-year-old daughter.

> An older Jewish grandmother is sitting alone on a park bench when a dissolute and sinister-looking, heavily tattooed man suddenly sits down beside her. She asks where he is from, quickly adding that she sits on the bench every day and has never seen him before. He says, in a low, muttering, intimidating voice, "I just got out of prison." "For what?" the old Jewish lady asks. "I killed my wife," he says. In an enthusiastic, Yiddish-inflected voice, she responds, "Ohhh, you're single!"

The fact that the man is undesirable, a convicted wife murderer no less, makes the joke funny. And yet this is another joke about the loss of Jewish identity. The Jewish grandmother is interested in someone as a potential husband, if not for herself, then, more likely, for a daughter or granddaughter, even if the single man is a wife killer. The single man also likely is not a Jew, given his tattoos; and his status as an ex-con does not make him a promising marriage prospect. The joke is, pointedly, about marriage as an end in itself for Jews.

Marriage is a form of *naches*. The meaning of many jokes, like the last one, is that Jewish mothers or grandmothers will do whatever it takes to find whatever can *shep naches* (provide pride and joy). It is best, of course, with a husband who is Jewish, and better yet, with one who is successful. But the joke suggests *naches* must be attained at any cost. A potential husband is a potential husband.

Saul Bellow's great, sprawling, award-winning Jewish American novel *The Adventures of Augie March* was originally titled *Life Among the Machiavellians,* meaning those for whom the ends justify the means. The title applied mainly to the men in the novel but could as easily have been applied to the character of Grandma Lausch. She is not the biological grandmother of Augie and his brother Simon, but like a true Machiavellian Jewish grandmother, she will do whatever it takes to see that the children in her charge are cared for. She places a premium on education and, if necessary, is tough and tyrannical in the pursuit of a single end—making the brothers into mensches. This is where Jewish mothers and grandmothers appear to excel, and it is what has made them—and continues to make them—objects of love and admiration as well as targets of ridicule for the anxiety and guilt they engender. You have the four Jewish grandmothers who are having lunch together in a restaurant when the waiter walks up to their table and asks, "Is anything all right?" Or the joke about the beggar who tells a Jewish grandmother he hasn't eaten in a week, and she says: "Force yourself."

If you delve deeply into the often-stereotyped portraits of Jewish mothers and Jewish grandmothers that emerge from the wide and disparate pool of jokes about them, you discover as much exasperation as you do recognition of the central part they play in shaping futures and forging lives.

Let's not forget the classic one-liner about the Jewish mother who sends a telegram that reads: BEGIN WORRYING. DETAILS TO FOLLOW.

"MY NAME IS TONTO GOLD-STEIN"

Sex & Marriage

A man looks at a scraggly and bedraggled parrot he sees in a cage at a pet store. The owner of the pet store tells him he can have the parrot for a couple of bucks but warns him that the bird, a female, says only one word. Soon the man hears the female parrot squawk the one word, repeating it over and over: "HORNY." The man pays the owner two bucks, takes the parrot, in its worn and rotted cage, home with him, and finds a friend waiting for him in his driveway. The friend, naturally, asks about the parrot and is told of its single-word vocabulary, which, soon enough, the friend hears as the parrot again squawks, "HORNY," and repeats it again and again. "HORNY. HORNY." "Listen," says the friend. "I know a guy who has parrots that daven and say Hebrew prayers all day long. Why don't we take your parrot and expose her to them? She can learn to say pious and holy words instead of constantly saying 'HORNY.'" The owner of the parrot is dumbfounded and cannot believe there are really praying parrots, but he goes along with his friend. They drive over, with the parrot, to the home of the man who owns the davening parrots. Sure enough, once they get inside the house, the parrot owner sees two parrots in a cage with small skullcaps on their heads and lovely little tallises, prayer shawls, draped across their feathers. It is incredible! Unbelievable! The two parrots, on top of their perches, are swaying back and forth, muttering Hebrew words in unison, in deep prayer. "Let's do it," says the owner's friend, and the owner takes the female parrot out of her cage and puts her in the cage with the two pious, praying parrots. No sooner is the female parrot in the cage than she squawks, "HORNY," and the two male parrots stop praying and together shout, "OUR PRAYERS HAVE BEEN ANSWERED."

It is the night of the marriage of a young Orthodox man. He seeks advice from his rabbi about the wedding night. "Rabbi," he begins, somewhat flustered and embarrassed, "I'm afraid I have three questions. I need to know, first, if it is okay for me to have relations with my wife doing what they call doggy style." A wise and compassionate man of erudition, the rabbi goes to his voluminous bookshelves and takes down one of the tomes. "Right here, in the twelfth century, Rabbi Yitzhak ben Gashtroodle says it is not only okay to have sex with your bride in that way, it is a *machaya!*" "Good," says the young man. "But what about doing it with my wife on top of me." Unblinking, the rabbi takes another volume from the shelf, opens it, and announces to the answer-seeking groom, "Here it is in black and white, going back to the ninth century. Rabbi Akiva Pupik says it is good to have one's bride on top on the wedding night, a blessing." "Fine," says the young man. "Then I only have one final question. What about our doing it standing up?"

Outraged, the Orthodox rabbi shouts, "Standing up? Absolutely not! That could lead to dancing!"

F OR PRACTICING Jews, marital sex has always been a mitzvah, both a commandment and a good deed, and the subject of sex has long provided grist for Jewish humor and Jewish jokes. Much of the material is based on stereotypes of oversexed men; passive, cowed, and docile husbands; and undersexed women, domineering wives, and Jewish American princesses. Much also has changed thanks to the work of feminists, many of whom have been Jewish, such as Betty Friedan, Bela Abzug, Susan Faludi, Naomi Wolf, and Gloria Steinem. Though I have interviewed all of these women, I know Gloria best. We have become friendly through numerous interviews over decades. I used to call her my "landsperson" instead of landsman. (A landsman refers to someone who originates from the same region or territory as you do.) Gloria is from Toledo and I am from Cleveland. But she informed me after one of our interviews that her mother was Presbyterian and she herself knew little about Judaism or Jewishness until she left Toledo.

Joan Rivers, early on, had a quiverful of self-deprecatory, well-delivered lines, rendered with aggressive gusto, about her lack of sex appeal, like the one about prison guards using nude pictures of her to curb the sex drive of men on death row. Or, as she aged, her line about wearing open-toed shoes to show off her breasts. A good deal of the humor of Jewish women has been tied to sexual self-deprecation. Years later, comic Amy Schumer would respond on air to Jon Stewart showing a photo of her on a boat with the actress Jennifer Lawrence, her reported BFF, saying she (Schumer) looked like Alfred Hitchcock.

As she became more successful, Joan Rivers became more aggressive (and blue) on the show *Fashion Police,* where she still made jokes about herself but, more often, launched verbal grenades at other celebrities, not all of them in very good taste. She would hit multiple targets with just a single photo—a picture of the singer Justin Bieber with his then girlfriend Selena Gomez goes on-screen and Joan comments: "Some things just do not go together. Like Britney Spears and books. Or Kim Kardashian and white penises." This type of outrageous humor, which many find vulgar, has its American roots. As Rivers often pointed out, these roots go back to the work of the Jewish comic Lenny Bruce and, later, the Jewish radio comic and self-proclaimed king of all media, Howard Stern. As Joan got older her humor became increasingly risqué and over-the-top—as if to shout out that she could be as crude as guy comics. She could also simultaneously ridicule the changing nature of the double standard in such one-liners as: "A man can sleep around, no questions asked, but if a woman makes nineteen or twenty mistakes, she's a tramp." She did revert to self-deprecatory Jewish humor, however, when she returned to *The Tonight Show* as a guest of Jimmy Fallon (after having been excluded for years by Johnny Carson and Jay Leno). That night she announced that her last appearance on the show was "four nose jobs ago."

Men, too, can savage their sexuality, of course. The constantly suffering comic Richard Lewis claimed his self-esteem was so low that when he was in bed with his *girlfriend* he would fantasize that *he* was someone else.

But women with a sexual track record have long been the subject of Jewish jokes, as in the joke featuring a *shadchan*, the traditional Jewish matchmaker or marriage broker. The *shadchan* goes to see parents who are looking for a mate for their son. He tells the parents he has a young woman from a family of considerable wealth. She is a rare beauty and has a model's figure, is a marvelous cook and a great conversationalist. The mother asks, "Is she good with children? Will she be a good mother?" The *shadchan* assures the mother that the young woman loves children and will no doubt make a wonderful mother. The father and mother are delighted. Then the father, somewhat hesitantly, asks: "Do you have any idea if she will be good in *bed*?" The *shadchan* hesitates, muses, rubs his chin, then says: "Some would say yes and some would say no."

When I interviewed Joan Rivers in 2010, I realized the impact her humor had had on women. As I escorted her out of the studio, we walked toward a queue of at least thirty women, who all worked in the broadcast building and had lined up to bow to her as she passed.

I asked Joan during our interview if anything was out of bounds for her and she said she reluctantly had decided not to tell a racial joke about first lady Michelle Obama. Otherwise, anything was permissible and no subject out of bounds, especially sexual ones. That proved to be the case when she created outrage by joking about the young Cleveland women held captive and abused for over a decade as sex slaves. According to Joan, they lived rent-free and were waiting for an invitation from *Dancing with the Stars*. No bounds, too, for Sarah Silverman, who once said she was raped by a doctor and added that the experience was bittersweet for a Jewish girl.

Traditional Jewish jokes and Jewish humor are often all about delivery and characteristically told more often by men. It was the speed and the cadence of shtetl-born Isaac Singer's Yiddish-inflected response to my question, in an onstage interview we did about free will (I asked him if he believed in it and he answered, "I have no choice") that the crowd found hilarious. The poor, henpecked husband's helplessness is the essence of many of Henny Youngman's rapid one-liners, the most famous being "take my wife—please!" Or take the Youngman joke, again told with a quick, jabbing, and aggressive delivery: *"My wife divorced me for religious reasons. She worshiped money. I didn't have any."* Jokes like this can lose a lot in the transition from oral to written.

The self-deprecation at the heart of much of Youngman's humor is the foundation, too, of Rodney Dangerfield's famous laments about getting no respect. But, again, even in jokes that ridicule his lack of sex appeal, the key to his success as a comic was tied to the telling, the delivery, with its Yiddish inflections and tone, the speed and "chic-a-boom" uplift at joke's end as well as the rapidity of one joke following after another. *"A woman I met told me to go to her house that night. She said no one would be there. I went. No one was there."*

Traditional Jewish jokes about dominated, passive hus-
bands are rooted in shtetl life. It was commonplace there (as it
still is among many of the ultra-Orthodox) for women to take
charge of nearly everything while the men studied Talmud
and Torah. Women in the shtetl were, in fact, often the sole
earners of what little money the household possessed. They
were the ones who put bread on the family table, while the
patriarch of the family acquired more learning and presum-
ably became closer to God. There is one such joke about how
marriage may be exceedingly difficult for most men, but for a
Jewish husband it means never having to make a decision. Or
the joke about Jewish husbands getting along with their wives
if they simply wake up every morning and say, "I'm sorry." In
the words of Groucho Marx, "Man does not control his own
fate. The women in his life do that for him." Or consider the
joke about the young man who goes off to college and tells his
parents he has decided on a career as an actor and is thrilled
to be cast in his first play in the role of a Jewish husband. His
mother asks, "A role with no speaking part?" That joke re-
minds us of the one about why no Jewish wives are on parole
boards. The answer: they wouldn't let anyone finish a sentence.

On the one hand, there are Jewish jokes about passive hus-
bands, and on the other, there are jokes about aggressive and

horny Jewish men, often younger single men or middle-aged married ones.

Men are frequently presented in Jewish jokes as being out of control sexually. As Billy Crystal once put it, "Women need a reason to have sex. Men just need a place."

In much Jewish humor, Jewish men of all ages have been presented as being as drawn to shiksas as Ulysses was to the Sirens—except, unlike that Greek hero, often there was nothing to restrain their lust and ardor, no masts to tie them to. "Shiksa" is a word that, thanks to characters like Elaine in *Seinfeld* and Charlotte in *Sex and the City*, has become nearly commonplace in referring to a female non-Jew. But the original meaning of the word is far more pejorative. Which, perhaps, helps explain how Gentile women often became highly sexually appealing to Jewish men. It became, however, more acceptable over time for non-Jewish men to wed Jewish women, doubtless because of Jewish identity being passed down through the mother rather than the father. The beautiful biblical queen Esther of the Purim story married the Persian king Ahasuerus, a Gentile, and was, as a result, able to save her fellow Jews from the murderous Haman. Esther stayed Jewish. By contrast and against her father's wishes, Shylock's daughter,

Jessica, marries Lorenzo and converts to Christianity in Shakespeare's *The Merchant of Venice*.

Jewish men, during the Nazi era, were often pictured as sexual predators of snow-white virgin Aryan beauties, a stereotype brilliantly satirized in Philip Roth's *Portnoy's Complaint*. Nazi propaganda was filled with pictures of gross-looking, stooped-over, hook-nosed Jews lusting after blond fräuleins. An episode of *Seinfeld* was all about the unstoppable sexual desire for Gentile women, or what was called shiksappeal, taking possession of Jewish men of all ages, even a rabbi. Elaine portrayed the alluring and irresistible shiksa, played by Julia Louis-Dreyfus (who despite being a descendant of the French army officer Alfred Dreyfus, of the infamous Dreyfus Affair, does not identify as being Jewish).

I interviewed Larry David onstage for a fund-raiser for the environmental action group NRDC. Julia was there. "I'm here for Larry," she told me. He was there for Laurie David, then his wife, who was also a major environmental activist and a trustee of the NRDC, as well as one of the producers of the film about global warming *An Inconvenient Truth*. I asked David why he decided to make his television wife Cheryl, played by Cheryl Hines, a shiksa rather than a Jew, like his then real wife, who was seated in the front row with their two daughters and Julia; he told me he had such a perfect Jewish wife in real life that he felt he could give himself a Gentile one on his HBO series. Once he and Laurie were divorced, Jay Leno had the temerity to ask David how he felt about the divorce and David made a joke about finally being able, with his environmentalist wife out of the picture, to take long showers.

David's response reminded me of the old Jewish joke that answers the question "Why is divorcing a Jewish woman so expensive?" The answer: "It's worth it." Once again we are dealing, obviously, with stereotypes, in this case of the overly dominating and restricting Jewish wife. Many find such stereotypes odious. But they can apply not just to wives—as we see in the joke about the woman who divorces her husband after seventy-five years of marriage. When asked by the judge why she was suing for divorce after three quarters of a century, she exclaims, "Because enough is enough!"

There is something in these types of jokes that elicits laughter, often laughter tied to the recognition of stereotypes. The stereotype of the harpy Jewish wife can be seen written large in the character of Susie, played by Susie Essman, in the series *Curb Your Enthusiasm*. This is a woman who screams, "You fat fuck," at her husband, Jeff. She upbraids, nags, and taunts him constantly, but is somehow still worthy of affection and even admiration from many who appreciate her toughness of character (especially because her husband is often engaging in morally questionable and sneaky or juvenile behavior). She is also presented as a loving, overly protective Jewish mother, though her daughter is somewhat conniving and sneaky like Jeff.

Yes, Jewish wives are often maligned in jokes, many centered around husbands who are sexually dissatisfied or believe their wives favor material things over them. A Jewish man asks to be cremated and have an urn of his ashes placed in Bloomingdale's since he knows his wife will visit him often. Or the Jew who dies and his widow is told she must pay by the word for his obituary in the local newspaper. She submits to the newspaper—*"MORT DIED. VOLVO FOR SALE."* (Other versions have a Lexus or a Cadillac.) I used to suspect these kinds of jokes emanated from Jewish husbands who felt their wives did not care enough about them, appreciate them, or pay enough attention to them, a kind of perverse way of making themselves into martyred victims. If a Jew dies in the forest, will his wife go shopping? The Jewish wife's perfect house? Six thousand square feet with no master bedroom and no kitchen.

An Italian man, a Frenchman, and a Jew are comparing notes on their marital sex lives. The Italian tells of a time he put olive oil all over his wife's body and made love to her as she screamed in ecstasy for five full minutes. The Frenchman counters with a tale of how he rubbed sweet butter all over his wife's body and made love to her, after which she screamed with delight for a solid twelve minutes. The Jew then relates how he rubbed schmaltz (chicken fat) all over his wife's body, made love to her, and then was screamed at for an hour and a half because he wiped his hands off on the drapes. (In another version he wipes a more intimate part of his anatomy on the drapes and she is still screaming as he relates the story.)

Jewish wives can be portrayed not only as low in libido but as insufferable nags, and all too often the portrayals are laced with venom. But even more often, we find that they are portrayed, like Jewish princesses, as spoiled and demanding.

If the Jewish wife is spoiled—and there are many jokes about people of all classes and varieties of backgrounds wanting to be reincarnated as a Jewish wife—who is the one spoiling the wife (or princess daughter)? The credit goes, of course, to the patriarch, the paterfamilias or head of the family who brings home the not-necessarily-kosher bacon. The real message in many of the jokes about Jewish wives, which, I believe, is also true of many of the Jewish American princess jokes, is not only that the Jewish women in them are provided for but that they can be tough and willfully independent of their husbands, the antithesis of geishas or Stepford wives.

A woman, Rita, is beyond consolation over the death of her husband, Marty. After months of grief, and in desperation, she goes to see a medium, who assures her that she can make contact with her late husband. Rita wants to believe the medium, but after a good deal of the medium's attempts to summon Marty's spirit, nothing occurs. That is, until the medium begins to speak in a voice like Marty's and calls Rita by endearing pet names no one outside their marriage could possibly know. Rita is thrilled and excited, nearly beside herself, certain she is actually communicating with her dead husband.

"Marty! Dumpling!" she shouts, as if she needs to be more audible to be heard. "What is it like for you on the other side? Tell me, Pumpkin!" Marty, through the medium, tells her that each day is like the one before. He wakes up, eats, *schtups,* and then goes to sleep. Then he eats again and *schtups* again and goes to sleep again, all repeated many times each day for seven days a week. "It's great," says Marty through the medium. "It sounds great," Rita repeats. "I am so happy you are happy in heaven, even if you are *schtupping* other women." Marty's voice comes once more out of the medium and he says, "Heaven? Other women? Who said anything about heaven or other women? I'm in Missouri. I'm a rabbit."

In some versions of this joke, Marty is a bull in Montana or a bear in Yellowstone. The animals, regardless of what they might be in the animal kingdom, are Jewish. A good deal of such humor, of course, like the horny male parrot joke, is in the absurdity of anthropomorphizing and giving Jewish qualities to animals. There is, in addition, perhaps a kind of latent wish for the nature of Jews or Jewish identity to be transmuted to other of God's creatures. But the real wish underlying this joke is for a man simply to *schtup* (have sex) all day, eat, and sleep for what may be eternity.

Jews as animals, by the way, is an ongoing literary tradition from Kafka's Gregor Samsa turning into a dung beetle to Bernard Malamud's talking Jewbird and Art Spiegelman's mice. But notice how Jewish jokes with animals often have to do with transgressive and forbidden behavior—horniness and adultery especially.

A sheep serves such a sexual purpose in an early Woody Allen film *Everything You Wanted to Know About Sex*. Gene Wilder portrays a doctor who has fallen madly in love and is carrying on an adulterous affair with a sheep. His wife finds out and he loses not only his marriage, but all his life savings. He even loses the sheep, who sends him a Dear John letter. He becomes, in fact, a down-and-out schlemiel, suffering misery alone and in disgrace and feeling shame over the loss of his woolen true love. At first, he works as a waiter in order to earn a living, wailing at the customers he serves that he used to be a doctor. Finally, he becomes utterly lost and forlorn.

Gene Wilder told me in an interview that it was a challenging role for him because he had to play it with complete seriousness, even when ordering champagne and caviar as well as grass (the kind that you mow not smoke) from room service in the hotel room he shared with the sheep. Wilder, whose real name is Jerry Silverman, and who, before my interview with him, was married to famed comic Gilda Radner, told me he learned at Lee Strasberg's Actors Studio the importance of playing comedy just as naturalistically as drama. The same Woody Allen film, incidentally, includes a rabbi being whipped by a beautiful blond shiksa while forced to watch his wife eat pork.

A Jewish man, Ben, and his much younger wife, Holly, are both troubled by the absence in her of much if any arousal or excitement in the bedroom. She is completely nonorgasmic. They decide to consult their rabbi, known for his compassionate counseling and, surely just as important, for his reputed proven track record for finding workable solutions to marital problems.

The rabbi proposes a plan. Ben and Holly should make love later that same evening at ten o'clock and the rabbi will see to it that a handsome young man in his congregation named Paul will be sent there before the action between the two begins. The rabbi will arrange it all. Handsome and muscular young Paul will stand naked before Holly and wave a towel back and forth while husband and wife are engaged in sexual relations. Holly, the rabbi hopes, will get excited and the lovemaking will get a much-needed game changing charge.

Unfortunately, the naked young man waving the towel in front of Holly has little or no effect and does not arouse her at all.

The couple go back the next day to see the rabbi. He is deeply concerned. "Let's have you try something else," he says to them. "It may sound quite radical, but it may turn things around. Let's have Ben trade places with Paul. In other words, Paul will make love to Holly and Ben will stand there naked and wave the towel."

They do as the rabbi suggests and Holly screams and howls in ecstasy as she has a number of convulsive orgasms with young Paul while a naked Ben waves the towel and shouts to Paul , "Now, that's how you wave a towel, boy!"

The real theme of this joke, of course, is sexual competition. Though the younger man has the obvious virility advantage, the Jewish husband is still trying to show that he is the better man, more potent and adept at his personal brand of towel waving. It's a bit of a dark comic joke because clearly the older husband does not have what it takes to satisfy his younger wife. But he tries!

There are many jokes about Jewish men competing with each other. In fact, there is an old saw about how every Jew thinks he can tell a better Jewish joke than the one who is telling the joke. A story comes to my mind about Jewish men competing with each other and a couple of Hollywood shiksa starlets on top of it. (Someone needs to do a book on all of the Jewish men who have been involved with or married to shiksa starlets).

The novelist Ethan Canin called me one day and asked if I wanted to see which of us could lose more weight in a week at twenty dollars a pound. I told him I wasn't interested. Soon after he called to tell me to look at an interview with the actress Helen Hunt in the then new issue of *Vanity Fair.* In it, Helen Hunt was asked what her ideal way would be to spend a day. Her response: "Hanging out with the author Ethan Canin." I called Ethan and told him I read what she had said and he immediately challenged me: "Go ahead and try to top that!"

I thought his challenge juvenile but a few weeks later two events occurred within a single day. Sydney Goldstein, who runs City Arts and Lectures in San Francisco, called to tell me she had lunch with famed novelist Umberto Eco. I had interviewed Eco that morning on my radio program. "He said you were a genius of an interviewer," she reported. Then, later that afternoon, I kept an appointment with filmmaker Barry Levinson at his home to discuss an event at a film festival where I would be interviewing him. As he led me toward the screening room in his home, he told his aide, "Hold my calls. I'll be with Michael." So I wrote Ethan an email saying "Umberto Eco called me a genius and Barry Levinson said, 'Hold my calls. I'll be with Michael.' You top that!"

Soon after I got an email from Canin telling me to check out the Sunday *New York Times* crossword puzzle. There I saw one of the puzzle items asking for the author of *Emperor of the Air*, Ethan's acclaimed first book of short stories. The email ended with "Top it!"

This, I thought, was getting silly. But a week later a mutual friend of mine and the then *San Francisco Chronicle* editor Phil Bronstein called to invite me and my wife to dinner at his home. Phil had just started dating (and would later marry) the film actress Sharon Stone, who had created a sexual sensation in her starring role in *Basic Instinct*. I wrote Ethan: "I had dinner with Sharon Stone."

Ethan wrote back: "Game over!"

As Jewish men age in Jewish jokes, they often become increasingly less potent and less libidinal. Take the following jokes:

A ninety-year-old Jewish man has a fifty-year-old wife. His wife yells to him from upstairs in the bedroom of their house, "Come upstairs and make love to me." He faintly yells back, "I can't do both."

An elderly Jew brags about having sex with his wife "almost every night," meaning, literally, almost having sex every night.

A son sends his aged father a nubile, attractive prostitute in a G-string. She asks if he is ready for "Super Sex." The old man takes one look at her up and down and says, "I'll take the soup."

Nevertheless, jokes about Jewish male sexuality more characteristically emphasize sexual appetite or virility, celebrating it as vigorous and enduring for Jewish men, even in old age.

An old Jewish man wakes up a priest after midnight in the church sleeping quarters to tell him he is screwing a beautiful, young, twenty-two-year-old woman. The priest is stunned and appalled. He asks the old man: "You are obviously Jewish. I am a priest.

You woke me up to tell me this? Why? Why are you telling me this?" The old Jew enthusiastically shouts, "I'm telling everybody!"

A priest invites a rabbi to sit with him behind the screen as he listens to confession. The priest, with the rabbi also invisible and by his side, hears three attractive young women in succession, each confessing to adulterous acts three separate times over the past week. After each confession, the priest instructs the young woman to say a certain number of Hail Marys and put a twenty-dollar bill in the collection box. The priest then tells the rabbi he needs a drink and asks the rabbi to take over what he assures him is an obviously easy and repetitive ritual. When yet another lovely young woman confesses to the rabbi to having performed acts of adultery twice over the past week, the rabbi says, "Come back here. We got a special. Three for twenty bucks."

This joke, a version of which I first heard many years ago as a boy, puts the Jew (in this case a rabbi) in the immoral role but also turns him into a deal maker. The given in the joke—that a priest would allow a rabbi to sit in on confession and, even worse, have him take over so the priest can go for a drink—is a way of ridiculing the priesthood (and the goyim) as drinkers, while also showing that Gentiles, Catholics in this case, and Jews can be pals. (Bill Maher's mother was Jewish and his father Catholic. He was raised Catholic and claimed he would go to confession with his lawyer, Mr. Cohen.) Though the rabbi in the joke about confession is no better for going along with the priest's transgressions, he ultimately is the one who elicits the laugh, which is tied to his ability to take advantage of a favorable opportunity. The joke brings money and sex together in a way that implies that Jewish cleverness and manipulation can bring, if not actual sexual reward, the promise of it. The real truth in the joke rests on the importance of strategic and quick thinking, which many Jews like to believe is a part of Jewish character. On a deeper level, the joke indicates a change in interfaith relations. The rabbi and the priest are pals and obviously trust each other. At the heart of the joke is what used to be called the ecumenical spirit between Jews and Catholics—a coming together of the faiths, as evidenced, too, in the joke about the new Jewish/Catholic merger establishing a church called Our Lady of Perpetual Guilt. Or Jon Stewart saying how his wife's Catholicism balanced with his Judaism: they were raising their children to be sad. Or the joke about the rabbi and priest who are good enough pals to open up and confide in each other about past transgressions.

> The priest asks the rabbi if he ever in his life has eaten pork and the rabbi confesses that he once, as a youth, indeed did taste the forbidden meat. Whereupon the rabbi asks the priest if he has ever had sex and the priest admits he once did. The rabbi then says, "It's a hell of a lot better than pork, isn't it?"

> Rabbi Federman goes on a private vacation to Las Vegas. Just as he is unpacking in his room, after checking into the hotel, he is surprised to hear the phone ring. It is one of the temple trustees, David Hertzel. "Rabbi," says Hertzel, "there is a surprise for you. Open your hotel room door." Puzzled by this, the rabbi puts down the phone, opens the door, and sees, standing there in the hall, a tall buxom blonde in a bikini. Uncertain what all of this is about, he tells her

to come in and have a seat. He goes back to the phone and immediately asks, "What is going on, Hertzel?" Hertzel answers, "A few of us on the board thought you might want a little female companionship while you were on your vacation, so the blonde is our gift. Isn't she sensational?" Rabbi Federman explodes in anger. "Hertzel! What is it with you and the others? Don't you realize I am head of your congregation, the spiritual and moral leader, not to mention a married man with children? How could you stoop so low, you and the others, to do something like this to me? I am angry. I am humiliated. I am hanging up on you." Whereupon Rabbi Federman slams down the phone. The blonde, having witnessed all of this, gets up and starts to walk toward the door to leave. The rabbi shouts, "Wait! Where are you going? No one is angry at you."

While they were once seen as sages dispensing wisdom and even envisioning the future, there now are many jokes ridiculing rabbis, especially Reform rabbis, who, the jokes often suggest, act more today like oversexed bank branch managers or ignoramuses about Judaism. Much of this, of course, is exaggerated and untrue. You see a constant lampooning of rabbis in episodes of *Seinfeld* and *Curb Your Enthusiasm* as well as in a number of the earlier, more comedic films of Woody Allen, and the fiction of Philip Roth. There are even jokes among Reform rabbis or their congregants about how soporific rabbis can be. One Reform rabbi I know tells me that he and his colleagues joke about the size of their congregations by saying, "I have one that sleeps eight hundred" or another saying, "Mine sleeps twelve hundred." A Reform rabbi I know was actually presented by his congregation with a certificate making him a diplomate in the American Association of Anesthesiologists.

A few years back, I was in Las Vegas to play poker in a Texas Hold 'Em (minor league) poker tournament. I made it to the final table. At that table, with me and six others, is a man wearing a yarmulke. He tells me I look familiar and asks me if we have played poker together at the Venetian. I tell him I never played there. He asks about other casino venues where he might have seen me and I soon realize that this fellow is an inveterate poker player. I ask him why he wears a yarmulke. "Do you pray for better cards or try to make them holy?" I ask. "No," he says. "I am a rabbi."

"Well," I say, "times have certainly changed with rabbis playing in Vegas poker tournaments." I was about to ask the rabbi if he played on Shabbat because it was Friday morning and tournaments can run days on end, but at this point our conversation appears to have caught the attention of a few of the other players at the table. "Where is your congregation, Rabbi?" one of them asks. "Pittsburgh," the rabbi says. Suddenly I am transfixed. One of my nieces lives in Pittsburgh. It jolts me into the sudden realization that this rabbi officiated at the bar mitzvahs of two of her sons, my great-nephews, both of which my wife and I attended. I say aloud the full names of both great-nephews. "You bar-mitzvahed both, didn't you?" I say emphatically. The rabbi looks at me in disbelief. All of the other poker players are now looking at both of us instead of their cards. They know I live in northern California and they are trying to figure out this odd Jewish geography dialogue. I simply state, "I was there. At both. I'm their great-uncle."

A young Jewish woman goes to see a rabbinic sage. She tells him that both Yankele and Yossel are in love with her. Then she asks the rabbi, "Who will be the lucky man? Who will marry me?" The rabbi strokes his beard and ponders, then answers, "Yossel will marry you. Yankele will be the lucky man."

The rabbi is telling the young woman, who brags about the two men in love with her, that she is conceited and a future shrew. He is puncturing her self-inflation and lack of humility. This all has contemporary currency but is also a joke more out of a Jewish past when rabbis were more likely to be seen as fonts of wisdom. In times past, rabbis were even believed to be able to perform miracles and peer into the future. One thinks of the Baal Shem Tov, the mystical Ukrainian rabbi of the eighteenth century who is said to have been the founder of Hasidic Judaism. The closest modern equivalent to him would have to be Rabbi Menachem Mendel Schneerson, of the Orthodox Lubavitcher sect, who founded the Chabad movement and was believed by his followers to have been a visionary, and by many of them, to have been the messiah the Jews had long been waiting and praying for. Despite his having had the rather mortal affliction of prostate cancer, the followers of the Rebbe, as he was and is still known, wait for his return from the dead.

A small synagogue in Venice, California, has a sign that reads: THIS JEWISH RELIGIOUS HOUSE OF WORSHIP IS LIBERAL AND PROGRESSIVE AND WELCOMES ALL PEOPLE. A young Jewish man sees the sign and enters the synagogue.

A service is going on with a young woman rabbi conducting. The young Jew sees a few scattered congregants seated with their prayer books open. One of them is a highly attractive redhead. He is immediately strongly sexually attracted to her and sits down near her.

As the service continues the young man inches closer to the redhead until he is seated right next to her. He is clearly smitten and leans over close to her and says, literally in her ear, "I think you are by far the most beautiful woman I have ever laid eyes on. I want you." At this point, the rabbi races down from the pulpit and, with anger and apparent outrage, orders the young man to leave the temple immediately. The young man protests and reminds the rabbi of the sign outside welcoming all people and laying claim to being a house of worship both liberal and progressive. The rabbi says to him: "That's true. But you don't hit on the *rebbetzin*."

Now, the patriarchal religion of Abraham, Isaac, and Jacob, which once had temples with male rabbis' names attached to them, has become the home of many female, and even a number of lesbian, rabbis.

Yes, Jewish marriage has changed with the times—and not only via same-sex nuptials. Jewish couples of my parents' generation almost never divorced.

A rabbi I knew surprised me, in the early seventies, by confidentially telling me he was coming out of the closet as a gay man, at a time when that was unheard of, especially for a rabbi It brought out from me the knee-jerk response, "Are you sure?" Incidentally, he had asked me, before this disclosure, if I wanted to teach a course on Jewish writers at a JCC in San Francisco. I told him I was keen at the time on Yiddish writers but I suspected, especially in San Francisco, where Jews seemed to celebrate Christmas and to name their offspring after the living (complete with Roman numerals), that I doubted I could draw a minyan—the standard number of ten required in Judaism to hold a religious service. The rabbi told me to write a sexy or clever description of the course, and when I showed up for the first class in Yiddish fiction writers, I was, as we used to say back then, blown away by the turnout. There were at least a hundred eager-looking students. How could this be? I thought. How? Particularly because of what I had come to think of as the predominant number of *yekkas* in

San Francisco—*yekka* being the name given to overly assimilated, secular German Jews.

A young woman tapped me on the shoulder. "Dr. Krasny," she began. "I'm sorry to tell you, but there has been a mistake. You are, unfortunately, in the wrong room. This room was reserved for Dr. Melvin Krantzler, who is giving a course on Creative Divorce."

I went across the hall. There were five older people signed up for my course in Yiddish stories, which included videos and was titled Yids and Vids.

Many of the themes in real-life stories, such as this one, obviously parallel motifs in Jewish jokes. Trying to preserve the past and its values in America, where, to draw from the seminal Jewish American novel *The Rise of David Levinsky*, you "leave your *yichus* behind," is not an easy task. *Yichus* is the prestige that comes from learning, especially Talmudic learning. My experience wanting to teach Yiddish writers at the JCC was set against American trends or values—in this case, an overwhelming trend at that time of higher divorce rates.

Jewish-based anecdotes and Jewish stories can be nearly indistinguishable from Jewish jokes, and changes in mores and cultural standards can be the very essence of a joke, especially one tied to sex, as in Sarah Silverman's line about her sister being with two men in one night and hardly able to walk. "Can you imagine?" Sarah asked. "Two dinners!"

> A Jewish man is seated next to a gorgeous and voluptuous woman on an airplane. She is studying graphs and charts laid out across her lap. When the Jewish guy asks what she is studying she informs him that she is a sex researcher. "What," he asks politely, "is the nature of your research?" "Well," she responds, "I'm researching the size of male genitalia in different ethnic groups. I've discovered that Native American men have longer penises, greater in length, while Jewish men's sex organs are much wider." The Jew sitting next to her says, "I need to introduce myself. My name is Tonto Goldstein."

In truth, jokes about male penis size are more often identified with black men than Jews or Indians. Notwithstanding the joke about Jewish women loving circumcised penises out of an inability to resist anything with 10 percent off, Jewish women are more often portrayed as sex negative. This is particularly true in many of the unfortunately so-called JAP or Jewish American princess jokes. In contrast to male libidinousness, jokes about Jewish women emphasize their supposed lack of sexual drive. Woody Allen got in some trouble when he joked, early on in his career, that his then wife, Louise Lasser, of *Mary Hartman* fame, was given a ticket while driving. He claimed he knew it could not possibly have been for a moving violation. Don Rickles once claimed to Johnny Carson on *The Tonight Show*, in a joke that likely could not pass muster by today's commercial television standards, that Jewish women cry out during sex. According to Rickles, they yell, "Gucci! Gucci! Gucci!" Despite the offensive characterization as frigid and overly materialistic, the emphasis in Jewish women jokes is on their differences from other women:

Question: What three words will a Jewish American princess never hear? Answer: "Attention, Kmart shoppers."

A Jewish American princess is in Tiffany's examining an extremely expensive vase, holding it up to the light and looking at it from a number of different angles, when it slips out of her hands, falls to the floor, and crashes into hundreds of pieces. She holds her hand up and says, "I'M All RIGHT."

These jokes, including even more harsh ones, reveal similar motifs of so-called JAPs being greedy, loving shopping and money, and hating or not wanting sex. But, in these two examples—Kmart and Tiffany's—there is an implicit sense of celebration. There is a sense of how far Jewish women have managed to come in contemporary life to be able to avoid (and thus maintain separateness or a kind of chosenness) a cut-rate shopping place like Kmart, and instead afford a place like Tiffany's. A young woman being a princess or being treated like one, being vain enough (like the young woman at Tiffany's) to think only she matters, are ways of saying—exclaiming, really—that our young women, daughters, and wives have made it. The jokes are celebrations of Jewish success and prosperity, of having only the best for the tribe's young women, even if the jokes lean toward misogyny. Particularly when it comes to sex: *What do you call a Jewish porn film? Debbie Does Nothing.* OR: *What is the difference between an Italian American princess and a Jewish American princess? With the Italian American princess the jewels are fake and the orgasms are real.* OR: *What do you call a water bed belonging to a Jewish woman? The Dead Sea.* OR: *What do you call Jewish foreplay? Twenty minutes of begging.*

An old Jewish man is walking down the street one af-
ternoon when he sees a woman with perfect breasts.
He says to her, "Hey, miss. Would you let me bite your
breasts for $100?"

"Are you nuts?!" she replies, and keeps walking
away.

He turns around, runs around the block, and gets
to the corner before she does.

"Would you let me bite your breasts for $1,000?"
he asks again.

"Listen, you; I'm not that kind of woman! Got it?"

So the little old Jewish man runs around the next
block and faces her again.

"Would you let me bite your breasts—just once—
for $10,000?"

She thinks about it for a while and says, "Hmm,
$10,000 . . . Okay, just once, but not here. Let's go to
that dark alley over there."

So they go into the alley, where she takes off her
blouse to reveal her perfect breasts. As soon as he
sees them, he grabs them and starts caressing them,
fondling them slowly, kissing them, licking them,
burying his face in them—but not biting them.

The woman finally gets annoyed and asks, "Well? Are you gonna bite them or not?"

"Nah," says the little old Jewish man. "Costs too much!"

Of course the joke is just another sex joke. But the Jew in the joke is old and still a lover of breasts who wants nothing more than a free go at a beautiful, "perfect" pair. Jews getting what they want for free can be seen in other jokes:

The biggest dilemma and catch-22 for a Jew? Free pork.

OR, *Why do Jews have big noses? Answer: Because the air is free.*

Are these jokes teaching us that Jews are cheap? No doubt. Cheap-Jew jokes are, alas, as old (if not older) than Jewish sex jokes. But wanting and managing to get things for free can be enterprising, especially if, unlike the air, they are difficult to come by.

The fact is, the old Jewish guy in the breast-biting joke is enterprising, even if he is also deceiving and manipulative, and the joke also seems to suggest the misogynistic notion that every woman has her price. Still, his sexual appetite and his shrewdness at getting something for nothing set him apart and are, in the joke at least, part of his Jewishness. The joke is imparting wisdom about human nature and the lure of money at the same time that it is saying something stereotypical about Jewish character being ingenious and entrepreneurial enough to acquire something for nothing.

An Israeli finds a bottle washed up on the beach. He uncorks it, and lo and behold, a genie emerges. The Israeli is startled but delighted, especially when the genie informs him that he can ask for any wish to be answered. The Israeli takes a map of the Middle East out of his pocket, hands it to the genie, and says to him, "I want peace between all of the people of this region." The genie looks at the map, studies it with brows furrowed and a look of great concern and vexation. "This wish," he finally pronounces, "I fear, is beyond my powers. Do you perhaps have a second wish I might be able to grant?" The Israeli puts the map back in his pocket and muses. Then he says to the genie: "How about getting my wife to give me oral sex?" The genie reflects, then says, "Let me have another look at that map."

Yes, another joke highlighting the supposed lack of sexual largesse of Jewish wives. It does so by making a Jewish wife orally pleasuring her husband more impossible than peace between Jews and Arabs. The joke, like so many other Jewish jokes, evokes another. This one is about a man named Irv Weiss, who is dying of a terminal disease. All of the best medical doctors and specialists have told Weiss and his wife that he has, at best, a few weeks to live. But there is hope. Weiss's wife gets word of a physician, known as a global leader in new research in the fight against the disease that is killing her husband. She immediately makes an appointment to see him and discuss her husband's condition. The doctor, a kind and thoughtful man, tells Mrs. Weiss that he is reasonably certain that if she performs oral sex to orgasm on her husband at least twice daily over each twenty-four-hour period for the next few weeks, he will be cured. "I know it sounds strange and implausible," the doctor adds, "but we have clinical trials that have proven this actually can save lives." After dinner that same evening, Mrs. Weiss sits down with her husband and tells him she saw the world's leading expert in his disease to find out about new clinical trials. "What did he say?" her husband asks eagerly. Mrs. Weiss: "He said you are going to die."

Herschel the magician appeared to have the extraordinary ability to crack walnuts with his penis. He performed for many years in small circus tent shows in rural hamlets across the country, and even those who witnessed the act could not believe it was real. Most thought some illusion or sleight of hand must have been involved to make it seem as if he actually was cracking walnuts with his sex organ. How could anyone actually do that? Clearly it was impossible. Well, Sam Goldfine, an amateur magician, witnessed this feat in the late 1970s in a small town off of a highway in Nebraska and was flabbergasted. Sam was an expert at detecting tricks used by magic performers and knew, beyond a doubt, that there was no trickery or sleight of hand involved. Sam had never seen anything like it then or over the years that followed. Until he was traveling one day through a small town in Ohio and saw a circus sign with the words: SEE THE AMAZING MAGIC OF HERSCHEL.

"Could it be the same Herschel?" Sam wondered. "Performing the same feat after all these years? No! It is not possible!" Yet after he paid his admission to the circus and went into the tent with Herschel's name on it, Sam saw a man who unmistakably was the same Herschel of nearly forty years before—a lot older, obviously, with hair turned gray—but wearing the identical, now ragged bathrobe he had on the first time Sam had observed him. Except this time, instead of walnuts, there was a large coconut in front of Herschel.

Herschel disrobes, takes his manhood in hand, and lo and behold, he slashes the coconut into two halves! The people applaud, though it is apparent to Sam they are doing so mainly out of politeness. Obviously they do not believe what they have seen was real and clearly feel there must have been a trick behind it. Sam Goldfine knows better. It was real!

Sam approaches Herschel, who now has his robe back on and is readjusting it. Sam introduces himself, shakes hands with Herschel, then says, "I saw you perform that same incredible feat nearly forty years ago with walnuts." Herschel smiles and nods. "Yes. I used to use walnuts. Now my eyes aren't so good."

Celebration of Jewish male virility appears not only in the portrayal of a magician with a hammer-hard, nut-shattering penis. There is also the joke about the two Jewish men fishing off the Golden Gate Bridge. One of them says, "I have to pee," and he takes out his penis and then remarks on how cold the water is. The other says he, too, must pee, takes out his penis, and adds, "Yes and deep." I first heard that joke told about two black men fishing. It likely was appropriated by Jews, reflecting perhaps a wish, as can be seen in someone like Howard Stern, to have an enormously large penis. It reminds me of the one about the professor of medicine, Dr. Silverstein, who is showing his students how to work anatomically on a cadaver. The cadaver, he says, is that of a man named Goldberg. Silverstein and his students are mesmerized at the size of Goldberg's genitals (which Norm Crosby, Jewish king of malaprops, used to say some old Jewish ladies called Gentiles, as in "the Genitals are different from the Jews"). No one can believe the gargantuan size of Goldberg's penis. Dr. Silverstein decides to hack it off and take it home. He puts it in a large shopping bag. When he sees his wife, he says, "You aren't going to believe your eyes when I show you what I took home from work on a cadaver with students earlier today." He takes out the huge penis and holds it up for his wife to see. She screams, "Oh my God. Goldberg is dead!"

These kind of chauvinistic, wishful jokes about penis strength or size can be connected to other jokes about overall Jewish male strength. Like the one about an old Jew who applies for a job chopping down trees. The prospective employer looks skeptically at him and says, "You seem kind of ancient for this type of work. What *experience do you* have?" The old Jew immediately responds, "I chopped many trees down in the Sahara forest." The employer says, "You mean the Sahara Desert?" The old Jew: "That's what they call it now."

A man shows up at a brothel in Omaha and tells the madam that he is an Israeli and has been told that her house of pleasure has a young Israeli beauty. The madam says, "Yes. We are very lucky to have her. She is the highest paid of all the girls in the house." The man asks the price and the madam tells him a thousand, the room included. He agrees to pay the price and the stunning Israeli is summoned and introduced to him. She takes his arm and leads him to one of the house's private rooms. He pays her the thousand dollars and proceeds repeatedly to have wild and unbelievably hot sex with her and then informs her that he, too, is an Israeli. "From where?" she asks. "From Haifa," he says. "Really?" she exclaims. "I am also from Haifa! I still have family there. Would you by any chance know my brother? He is a dentist and his name is Baruch Holtzman." The man says to her, "Yes. I do know your brother. In fact, he cleaned my teeth just last week, and when I told him I was going to Omaha on business, he asked me to see if I could find his sister and return to her the thousand dollars he owes her."

In this joke we see, again, Jewish cunning with money in exchange for what amounts to free sex. Given the usual focus in jokes about Jewish wives on their lack of sexual desire, it surely ought to come as no surprise that Jewish men are often portrayed as going to see hookers for sexual relief or gratification. Take the one about the Jewish father walking down the stairs in a brothel who sees his son walking up. The son is shocked and stunned. "Dad! What are you doing here?" The father sheepishly responds: "Better to spend a few bucks here than bother your mother."

I don't know how common it was, but back in my day, at least a couple of the Jewish guys I knew were initiated into sex as boys by their fathers taking them to whorehouses. I could no more imagine my own father taking me to one than I could imagine him taking me to a church or a mosque to pray. Some of the miscreants I hung out with as a kid in Cleveland would go to houses of ill repute, though not with their dads. One of them, a guy we called the Duke, went one morning for oral satisfaction and was met by a rather large and obese hooker who told him she would service him for free. When he returned, he jubilantly told the guys he had free sex at the cathouse. They immediately convinced him, as a gag, that the hefty hooker was really a guy in a wig, something they made up on the spot to get him crazy. Easily provoked, Duke went back with his father's shotgun demanding to know if she was actually a she and ordering her to prove it. All pretty lurid and even grotesque by today's standards, but to adolescent Jewish boys, there was great mirth at having fooled Duke and made him temporarily go bonkers.

Some of those adolescent forms of humor can last a lifetime. My adolescence in Cleveland had much of the angst and Sturm und Drang associated with growing up, but there was much humor, a rich vein of it, especially associated with sex, in a club I joined when I was fifteen. The club was made up almost entirely of Jewish guys (one of the lone Gentiles in the club used to sing, to the tune of Paul Anka's "I'm Just a Lonely Boy," "I'm just a lonely Goy"). One of the club leaders, Duke's best friend, was a football player, a guy as strong physically and as good-looking as he was an inordinate bullshitter—but a very funny kid given to mocking nearly everyone he came in contact with, especially his friends. We called him B.S., and he went on to become a successful money manager and family man who never let up on the mocking.

I am with B.S., his wife, and a few other friends, in a coffee shop in Cleveland years after I left my hometown and moved on to California, a family of my own, and careers in academia, broadcasting, and writing. The problem with any success, however, with a guy like B.S., is that he will never let up on the sarcasm and ridicule. He will never cease letting you know who you once were or who he thought you were; he will never let you forget any sexual rejection or odd sexual experience you might have had that he thought he knew. While with him in the coffee shop, I happen to spot a copy of *San Francisco* magazine in a big rack of magazines. I ask B.S. to come with me to the rack. With a display of mild annoyance, he follows. I take out the magazine and open it to a photo of me standing next to the actor Ed Harris at the San Francisco International Film Festival, both of us in tuxedos. The caption reads: "Actor Ed Harris and Radio Polymath Michael Krasny." Can B.S. actually be impressed? He studies the photo, then looks at me and says, "So?"

"So?" I say. "Did you read what it says?"

"Yes," he grumbles. "I read it."

As if talking to a child, I ask, "What does it say?"

B.S. reads the caption with his usual tone of mockery.

"Do you know who Ed Harris is?" I ask.

"No," he answers, his voice laced with sarcasm, "I do not know who Ed Harris is."

"Well then. Do you know what a polymath is?"

Again in a voiced laced with sarcasm, "Yes. I know what a polymath is."

"What is it?" I ask.

"It's a fucking asshole."

A Japanese wife, Hiroko, is told by her husband that an anonymous source has informed him she is carrying on an affair with a Jewish man. Outraged and stung by the accusation, Hiroko responds, "Who told you such misheggass?"

The humor in this joke, of course, is in "misheggass," the Yiddish word for craziness. It is also in the sheer nature of the sound of that word—its euphonic force, in this case in a Japanese wife's use of it.

When Bill Clinton was president of the United States, a joke circulated that went: you could tell Clinton was crazy and truly out of his mind because he had a Jewish mistress and a Gentile lawyer. The joke is a combined JAP joke (Jewish women do not make good mistresses) and chauvinistic Jewish joke (but Jews are superior lawyers).

Poor Monica. This Jewish girl Hillary Clinton called a mall rat became marked for life as the girl who gave the leader of the free world oral sex. I was walking in downtown San Francisco around the time of the Lewinsky scandal, when a black street guy holding a sign that said I LEFT MY AFRICAN AMERICAN EXPRESS CARD AT HOME approached me asking me for spare change, and then suddenly, abruptly and vigorously, asked me, "What do you call an eight-day blow job?" The question caught my attention. I responded: "I don't know. What do you call it?" The street guy quickly shot back, "Hanukkah Lewinsky."

An older Jewish woman on an airplane, in first class, is seated next to an attractive younger woman. The younger woman looks at a ring on the older Jewish woman's hand and cannot help but tell her how extraordinary and beautiful it is. "I've never seen a larger or more beautiful diamond!" she exclaims. "Yes," the older Jewish woman says. She then confides, "It is worth nearly as much and is almost as big as the famous Hope Diamond. But just like the Hope Diamond, it carries a curse."

"A curse?" says the young woman fearfully. "What kind of a curse?"

"It goes back many years. It is called the Plotnick curse."

"Who or what is Plotnick?"

"Plotnick? He's my effing husband."

Why the name Poltnick appears in a number of Jewish jokes will always be a mystery, but the lesson this joke conveys about money not bringing happiness is clear. It is also about how difficult it must be for certain Jewish wives to abide the overly affluent men they choose to marry. Bernard Madoff's wife? Or Sheldon Adelson's? I have no idea. But the significant element in this joke is the candid and cathartic confession of a Jewish wife who has to endure her husband in addition to dispensing advice to the younger woman who can learn an important lesson: don't marry a rich man just for his money.

A Jewish husband is seriously injured in a car crash and is bandaged from head to toe. His doctor tells him the worst news is that his penis has been completely severed from his body and could not be found in the wreckage. The man emits horrible sounds of sorrow and loss until the doctor, trying to reassure him, tells him that there is a new artificial penis that is as good as a real one and will not cost him anything. His insurance will cover the ten-thousand-dollar cost of the new penis as well as the necessary surgery. The only remaining concern, the doctor says, is the fact that there are only two models. One is five inches and the other is ten—but the insurance will pay for either. He only has to choose. The physician adds, "You obviously will need to consult with your wife. Five may be too small for her and ten too large. So ask her and be sure to tell her the insurance will pay for whichever." A couple of days go by and the doctor revisits the Jewish husband. He asks him if he has had an opportunity to consult with his wife about which size penis to choose. The husband says, "Yes." The doctor then asks, "The five or the ten?" The Jewish husband answers, "We're getting granite countertops."

This is a classic whipped Jewish-husband joke. The man has no will of his own, even when he needs to replace his sex organ. The wife rules and the poor husband is apparently compelled to live a sexless life. These types of domineering-Jewish-wife jokes, once again, lampoon, hyperbolically, the strength and hegemony of Jewish wives and the extreme passivity of their husbands.

> A number of men who die enter heaven and are told to line up on the right if they did everything their wives told them to do and on the left if they didn't. A Jewish husband dies, enters heaven, and is given the same instructions. He sees a long line of men on the right and one lone man on the left. He cannot contain his curiosity. Walking up to the lone man on the left, who is wearing a yarmulke, he asks, "How come all of the men here are in line on the right and you alone are on the left?" The man with the yarmulke answers: "I don't know. My wife told me to stand here."

Jackie Mason tells of a Jewish husband returning home from a day at work as a big-shot lawyer or a much-respected doctor or CEO, only to hear his wife shout at him, "You schmuck! You forgot to take out the garbage!" Then Mason tells of an Italian husband coming home at three in the morning without explanation. His wife is stirring pasta and she says, "Hello, Tony. Please don't beat me." The henpecked Jewish husband versus the brutish Italian husband is not too difficult an opposition to deconstruct. Plus, the Jewish husband comes home straight from work while the Italian husband doesn't appear until 3 A.M. His wife stirring pasta at that hour and pleading not to be beaten by him speaks volumes about the perceived differences in the ways in which these wives are presumably treated and behave. Of course this is all ludicrous, hyperbolic, and absurd, but the real essence of the joking is that a Jewish husband may be ridiculed by his wife for his passivity, but, by clear implication, who is the better husband—the Italian or the Jew? And which wife is more admirable by today's feminist thinking— the tough bitchy one who calls her husband a schmuck or the passive, cowering one who lives in fear of him?

A Jewish man, sitting in a deli, notices a Jewish funeral. Two hearses go by with a man behind them walking a dog on a leash. A line of hundreds of men walk behind him. The Jewish man in the deli is curious. He walks toward the man walking the dog. When he reaches him, he tells him he has never seen a Jewish funeral with two hearses. The man with the dog tells him that one hearse is for his wife who yelled at him and was attacked and killed by the very dog he is walking. The second hearse, he says, is for his mother-in-law, who was attempting to help his wife, and was also attacked and killed by the same dog. The man from the deli offers his condolences and the two share a profound moment of male connectedness until the man from the deli asks if he can borrow the dog. The mourner replies, "Get in line."

Would you call that joke mean-spirited? Hostile? Dark? Misogynistic? Anti-marriage? Any one or all might apply. So might the famous words of Henny Youngman—"take my wife." In the joke, the guy just wants his wife dead. Man's best friend helps accomplish what the joke strongly suggests many married men (as seen by the long line of them) would like done. A single indignity is named—the wife yelled at her husband and the mother-in-law supported her daughter. Hence their joint fates.

These type of jokes are built not only on aggression, but also on fantasies of male freedom from marital oppression. The jokes are lethal for Jewish wives, as we see in the one about the band of three armed, masked robbers who take over a bank, insisting that all customers get down on the floor. One of the robbers walks around brandishing his weapon while the others hold up the tellers and put bundles of currency into bags. The robber walking around accidentally knocks his mask off. He picks it up, puts it back on, and says to one of the customers lying on the floor, "Did you see my face?" The customer says yes and the robber shoots and kills him. The robber then asks a second customer lying on the floor if he saw his face, and when that man admits he did, the robber shoots and kills him. The robber proceeds to a third man and asks the identical question: "Did you see my face?" This man quickly responds. "No. But my wife did."

A surgeon, just emerging from the operating room into the waiting room, meets a husband, a close friend of his and a golfing buddy, with a somber and sorrowful face. "You know how dicey this surgery was," the doctor says. The husband nods. "Well, we saved her. But the sad news is, she is a paraplegic for the rest of her life and will need constant care. Everything. Feeding. Eliminating. You'll need to change diapers and move her body around to avoid bedsores. She is going to require full-time care." The husband looks abject. Whereupon his surgeon buddy punches him lightly on the arm and says, "I'm just fucking with you. She's dead."

Nevertheless, Jewish-women comics do strike back when it comes to jokes like these. Consider the line from Elayne Boosler, who said, "My ancestors wandered lost in the wilderness for forty years because, even in biblical times, men would not stop to ask for directions." Or Roseanne Barr's tinged-with-murder line: "The way to a man's heart is through his chest."

A man named Lefkowitz has never transgressed even once in his life. He has performed countless mitzvahs. He dies and ascends to heaven. He is told by God's chief angel that his mitzvahs and his sin-free life are laudable and remarkable but not human enough for admission to an eternal reward. "Humans by nature sin," states the angel. In order to enter the kingdom of heaven, Lefkowitz will need to commit at least one single transgression. He will be extended a twenty-four-hour return to earth. Failing to sin at least one time will mean the gates to heaven will stay forever closed to him.

So Lefkowitz returns to earth and hours pass with not even a fleeting opportunity to sin until a middle-aged woman passes by and gives him an approving come-hither look. It is clear to Lefkowitz that the woman is sexually interested in him, so he goes up to her and awkwardly begins a stilted conversation.

She responds, and before he knows it, he has gone with her, at her invitation, to her apartment, where he winds up in bed with her. He completes the sex act and feels immensely relieved with the realization that the gates of heaven will now open for him until the woman says, "Thank you so much for making love to me. I've been feeling like an old lady lately and your lovemaking was a true mitzvah!"

This is a joke reminiscent of today's hookup culture, in which sexual relationships are initiated by the once-called "fair sex." Women more often are now pictured in jokes as being sexually aggressive, as in the one about the Hasid who bumps into a stunning woman by accident at a train station. She is blond and voluptuous and suddenly, unexpectedly, says to him: "I have my entire life had a fierce attraction to Hasidic men. I have a studio apartment only a couple of blocks from here. I would love to take you there and lick your body from head to toe." She goes on, with undisguised lust and ardor, to promise him whatever he might sexually desire. The Hasid looks her over, thinks about her offer of unbridled sexual pleasure, then asks: "What's in it for me?"

I don't know if the woman in the joke is supposed to be Gentile. A blond woman in a Jewish joke often turns out to be decoded as a shiksa. That, aside from obvious self-interest and sexual naïveté, may account for the Hasid being suspicious. Nevertheless, the woman is the sexual aggressor as she ardently offers any sexual gratification his Hasidic loins might want. Yet the Hasid in the joke still wants to know what he can get out of the deal. Which makes him a schmuck. Not a villainous schmuck. Just a plain schmuck.

If Jewish notions of sex and sexual roles and marriage are in flux—and surely no one would argue this not to be the case—many of the changes that have occurred or are occurring are mirrored in Jewish jokes. You could almost feel nostalgic to recall a gender joke like one from the great Jewish comedian Myron Cohen, who said, back when China was still referred to as "Red" China: while Jewish husbands solve world problems such as what to do about Red China, Jewish wives discuss how well red china goes with different-color tablecloths.

But let me bring this section on sex and marriage to a close by recalling a story that takes us back to "the decade of foreplay," as comedian Lily Tomlin called the pre-1960s sexual era. This is another one of those stories where joke and anecdote seem to converge. It concerns a lifetime friend of my dad's, perhaps his best friend, an amiable Jewish insurance salesman named Frank.

When he was young, Frank was known as "a nice Jewish

boy," not an uncommon designation even up to the present day. But the story is clearly of another era.

Frank was visiting, I suppose you could say he was courting, at the home of the girl he would eventually marry. There was a torrential downpour, which prompted the girl's parents to invite Frank to stay the night at their home rather than head back. Frank thanked them politely and agreed to spend the night. Then he left and ran into the rainstorm. He returned nearly an hour later totally drenched and carrying a paper bag. He had raced home to get his pajamas.

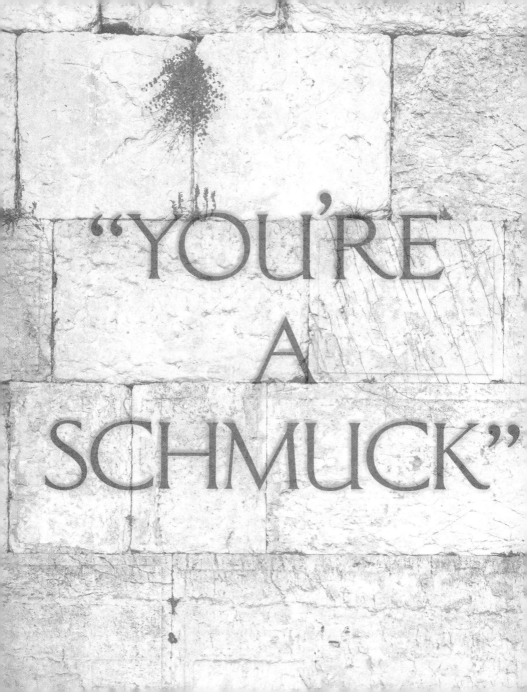

"YOU'RE A SCHMUCK"

III.

Schlemiels
& Schmucks

A bear manages to get into a cave and has a schlemiel cornered in it. The schlemiel cannot escape. Realizing this, he begins reciting the *shema,* the traditional Hebrew prayer praising Adonai, the one God Jews have worshiped for centuries. Suddenly, miraculously, he realizes that the bear is reciting the *shema* along with him, and he rapidly thinks to himself that the bear, incredibly enough, must be a Jewish bear. Then he hears the bear, in its deep bear voice, utter the prayer before eating: *"Ha motzi lechem min ha'aretz."*

An awful Jewish man, a real schmuck, dies. A ruthless man who had been unkind to his employees and even to his wife and children, he was a man of low character. But despite all his dark traits, he gave money to his synagogue, though largely for show. When he dies, the rabbi of his synagogue is approached by the schmuck's younger brother, who makes an offer. If the rabbi agrees to say that the deceased was a mensch at the funeral service, the younger brother will donate a million dollars to the synagogue's capital campaign.

The rabbi agonizes. The night before the funeral service he despairs to his wife, "A million dollars! You realize what that would do for our capital campaign? It would boost us right to what we need. But how can I say that *mamzer* was a mensch? He was a schmuck, a terrible, bad, dreadful human being. How can I possibly, in good conscience, call him a mensch?"

The next day, at the well-attended funeral service, the rabbi begins and intones: "I cannot lie before all of you here today. I don't even understand why so many have come to pay respects for such a man. He was ruthless and incorrigible and unkind. Frankly, he was cruel and dreadful. BUT COMPARED TO HIS BROTHER HE WAS A MENSCH."

THE FIGURE of the schlemiel has taken on many identities from its folkloric and archetyal character in the Ashkenazi Yiddishkeit (Yiddish culture) world of the shtetl to the world of the present day. Schlemiels are usually hapless bungling characters often barely able to make their way through life. A schlemiel can be lovable but he (never a she) is usually a dope or loser who frequently finds himself in absurd or troubled situations. Think Charlie Chaplin or the early Woody Allen. Or Isaac Bashevis Singer's Gimpel the Fool—a character in a classic Yiddish short story. Singer told me many people confused Gimpel with Gimbel, the name of the famous American department store—which made him consider, he said, writing a sequel to "Gimpel the Fool" titled "Macy the Idiot."

The schlemiel, above all, is indeed a fool, but one who needs to be distinguished from his Yiddish counterpart, the schlimazel. Someone no less than the great Jewish pitcher Sandy Koufax, after calling himself a schlemiel (hardly an apt self-description!) for refusing to pitch in a World Series game scheduled on Yom Kippur, gave the standard distinction to broadcaster Joe Garagiola. (In Cleveland, where I grew up, we pronounced the "Kippur" in Yom Kippur as if it were a fish). The standard distinction between the two famous characters is that the schlemiel is the guy who clumsily knocks over a bowl of soup; the schlimazel, meaning literally a person with bad luck, is the one the soup spills on. My dad, who was bald, returned one day from a ball game calling himself a schlimazel because, of all the people at Cleveland's municipal stadium, the bird, as he put it, "did its business on my head."

The schlimazel became a recognized figure in the United States with a character invented by Al Capp (née Caplin), the cartoonist who created Li'l Abner. The cartoon featured a poor soul named Joe Btfsplk, who had a constant cloud over his head and, though well-meaning and a loyal friend, was a jinx who had constant bad luck and brought it on others. The schlimazel, like the schlemiel, can be likable, even lovable, and one can feel tenderness toward him. But both characters, especially the schlizmazel, are losers; more successful men typically do not want to hang out or do business with them. When I think of schlimazels in that vein, I think of the so-called coolers who are said to bring bad luck to gamblers if they are anywhere near where gambling is going on. I sometimes also think, though his tragedies and losses are God's doing, that Job, in the Bible, may be the Ur-schlimazel.

Schlemiel and schlimazel became distinct in American popular culture with the lyrics to the theme of the sitcom *Laverne & Shirley,* which aired from 1976 to 1983: "One, two, three, four, five, six, seven, eight, schlemiel, schlimazel, hasenpfeffer incorporated." Sung by a group of kids, the lyrics were from a hopscotch song that Penny Marshall, who played Laverne, had learned as a girl growing up in the Bronx. Her brother Garry created the show, as well as *Happy Days, Mork and Mindy,* and a number of major movies such as *Pretty Woman, Runaway Bride, Beaches,* and *The Princess Diaries.* He also cast the comic George Burns, who was Jewish (née Nathan Birnbaum), as God in the film *Dear God.* Marshall himself played a number of Jewish characters, including Stan Lansing on *Murphy Brown,* which ended its ten-year run in 1998. Nearly everyone, including me, thought Marshall was Jewish, but he was born Garry Masciarelli, baptized Presbyterian, and raised Lutheran, which sounds a bit like the setup for a joke.

When I think of schlemiels, I think about the writer who

was often called the Yiddish Mark Twain, Sholem Aleichem, who created schlemiels in his fiction and remains most famous for the Tevye stories, which were the basis for *Fiddler on the Roof.* When that world-famous musical first came to Broadway, the lines were long enough for Norman Mailer to comment wryly to me about all the fascist Jews looking for shtetl nostalgia. Why fascist Jews? Because, for Mailer—who also once told me that the last thing in life he ever wanted to be called when he was young was a nice Jewish boy—"fascist Jews" referred to the bourgeois and well-heeled Jews who could now afford a Broadway show, many of whom were likely supporters of the war in Vietnam, and had clearly become (to use a great H. L. Mencken word) "bourgeoisossified." The irony was that wealthy Jews were paying to see a show focused on their poor and persecuted ancestors. Yet his comment was, to me, also a yardstick by which to measure how far many Jews had come from the penury of the shtetl. It brought to my mind a gold-laden bowl I saw once when visiting the Hamptons. Inside the bowl, inscribed in gold: "Nouveau is better than no riche at all."

One of Sholem Aleichem's best-known stories, "On Account of a Hat," is instructive about schlemiels. The protagonist is a poor Jew on his way home for Passover. Sholem Shachnah accidentally picks up a hat belonging to a Russian official and puts it on his head. He soon finds himself being treated with great respect and deference, being put in a first-class train compartment, and repeatedly being called "your excellency." The entire Jewish community of Kasrilevke discovers this story and feasts on the humor for days and weeks, especially the children.

A folktale similar to the Sholem Aleichem one is about the schlemiel in czarist Russia who desperately needs a bed one night and is surreptitiously brought in by a fellow-schlemiel hotel operator to sleep in a bed next to a sleeping Russian general. By mistake, the schlemiel puts the general's uniform on the next morning, quietly sneaks out of the room, and thinks at first, when he is outside the hotel and sees nothing but sycophantic and obsequious salutes and fawning deference, that something must have rubbed off on him from sleeping next to the general. That is, until he sees his reflection in a mirror, clad in the general's uniform. He is such a loser, dummy schlemiel that he believes it must be the general in the mirror while he must still be oversleeping in the hotel bed.

Schlemiel folk humor is embedded in the stories of the so-called wise men of Chelm. They sold books about how to read. By the same token—if schlimazels sold umbrellas, we are told, the sky would cease raining. If they sold shrouds, people would stop dying.

Most Jews, given the choice, would likely identify them-
selves or their loved ones as being schlemiels, or even schlima-
zels, rather than schmucks. Schmucks are not lovable, or usually
even likable, though they can be appealing, even charismatic.
They are everywhere. Look at the success of movie portraits of
greedy schmucks or schmuck con men who happen also to be
Jewish. They are no longer hidden from plain view, especially
after the true characters of Irving Rosenfeld and Jason Belford
were brought to life by Christian Bale and Leonardo DiCap-
rio (neither one a Jew) in the major motion pictures *American
Hustle* and *The Wolf of Wall Street*. Philologists will continue
to argue over what the word "schmuck" really means—the
Yiddish word actually, literally, means penis, and it is as pejo-
rative in its original meaning to call a man a schmuck as it is
to call a woman "the C word." But a less successful film called
Dinner with Schmucks tried to ally the word to idiots or hapless
tools. It has long been a word connected more to men of low
character, deserving of contempt.

You pretty much have to be Jewish to be labeled a schlemiel.
But nowadays anyone can be called a schmuck. The unlikely
team of comedian Jackie Mason and famed divorce lawyer
Raoul Felder wrote a book called *Schmucks!* about "fakes,
frauds, lowlifes, and liars," which includes in it a schmuck
hit list, a targeted selection of those the politically biased co-

authors deemed worthy of this Yiddish *S* word, ranging from
Mel Gibson, the Clintons, Al Sharpton, Al Gore, Barbara Strei-
sand, Madonna, and Katie Couric to the country of France.
But, like so many words, "schmuck" has evolved and come to
have manifold meanings. It still can mean a prick, but it has
become more identifiable with someone who acts like a jerk,
someone worthy of disdain. Young people today would call the
guy a dick.

Lenny Bruce once claimed his infamous arrest for profanity
was the result of having been heard using the word "schmuck"
by a Yiddish-speaking undercover cop. The word was vulgar
and profane then, but later on morphed into a kind of all-
purpose pejorative. A slew of Yiddish words beginning with
the "schm" sound are pejorative (as are many English words
that begin with the "sn" phonetic sound). Think schmendrick
(the one who cleans up the soup that was spilled by the schle-
miel onto the schlimazel); schmegegge (often used to describe
a lowlife or a person who is full of hot air or B.S.); *shmata* (a
lousy or unflattering piece of clothing). Initially, calling some-
one a schmuck was simply, in effect, calling the person a prick.
It was, in that sense, comparable to the word "putz," which
also has come more to mean a fool or would-be big shot but
originally meant a penis (as in the old question: *How do you
play bedroom golf? The answer: You sink your putz.*)

Despite all of the semantic confusion over schmuck, Mel Brooks tried defining it by saying, "You can be a poor schmuck, a lazy schmuck, a dumb schmuck, or just a plain old schmuck. A group of people can be collectively referred to as schmucks. You can call someone a schmuck, and you can be called a schmuck. You can even call yourself a schmuck." In 2007, Brooks claimed he was starting a nonprofit foundation to save the word from obsolescence or extinction, plaintively confessing that he did not want to live in a world in which "schmuck" would be replaced by words such as "prick," "jerk," or "douchebag." He made a point of urging people to call up their friends and loved ones and tell them, "You are a bunch of schmucks." He also said, near tears, that he had never before revealed it to anyone, but his father was a schmuck.

A down-and-out actor, a schlemiel named Moishe, reluctantly takes a job he finds in a classified ad as an ape impersonator. It turns out that the job is at New York's Central Park Zoo and has come about because of budget cuts that prohibit the zoo from buying another ape to replace one that has just died. So Moishe is hired and his job is to act like a real ape inside a cage during all of the zoo's open hours. Initially, he feels uncomfortable in the role he must play and guilty about deceiving the public. But soon he takes to it with gusto and hangs each day from the bar in his cage, swinging on vines, devouring bananas, and roaring and beating on his chest like King Kong. He begins to draw crowds until, one day, while swinging on the vines, he loses his grip and sails over the fence into the lions' cage right next door. Staring the lion right in the eyes, face-to-face, he recites the *shema* in mortal dread, "Hear, O Israel. The Lord our God. The Lord is one." The lion roars back, "Blessed be his glorious name forever and ever." Whereupon, from a nearby cage, a panda shouts, "Will you two schlemiels shut up? You'll get us all fired."

It turns out man-eating Jewish bears, and even schlemiels dressed as animals, can all recite the shema.

Generally, schlemiels are afflicted by circumstances in which they are helpless or made to look like fools. They populate more Jewish jokes and tales than probably any other figure from Jewish folklore and they usually stand for or are identified with the hapless Jew of the shtetl. But in this joke they are simply contemporary actors out of work, obliged to pose and behave as animals to make a living wage.

Morris and Becky live above their small grocery store.

They are in bed, asleep, and Morris is fitfully tossing and turning. He bumps into his wife and wakes her up.

"What?" she asks.

"Oy," Morris says, "I'm so worried. I don't know how I'm going to pay Horowitz the ten dollars I owe him."

"Go back to sleep," says Becky.

Fifteen minutes later, Morris is again tossing and turning, and accidentally kicks Becky, waking her up.

"What now?" she asks.

"Oy, I'm so worried. I don't know how I'm going to pay Horowitz the ten dollars I owe him."

"Go back to sleep."

Another fifteen minutes go by and again Morris is tossing around, now catching Becky in the ribs with his elbow.

"What?"

"Oy. I'm so worried. I don't know how I'm going to pay Horowitz the ten dollars I owe him."

Becky leaps out of bed, stomps over to the window, and throws it open. Outside, it is the middle of the night, everything is dark and still. Becky shouts at the top of her lungs,

"HERSCHEL, HERSCHEL HOROWITZ! HERSCHEL HOROWITZ!"

Finally, on the other side of the street, a window goes up and a sleepy head appears. *"Nu,* so who wants me?"

Becky yells in a clear voice, "MORRIS GOLDFARB IS NOT GOING TO PAY YOU THE TEN DOLLARS HE OWES YOU."

She slams the window shut, stomps back to bed, and says, "Now let him worry. You get some sleep!"

Morris Goldfarb appears ethical, literally losing sleep over an unpaid debt. The joke is about a side of Jewish character— the overriding (and guilt-ridden) need to settle a monetary debt, an anxiety joke that reveals a man who obviously has a conscience. But Morris is also a schlemiel. He is a schlemiel because he seems totally lost and without a clue about how to handle paying off his debt and he, like many schlemiels, is woebegone. His wife, Becky, has to intercede and take charge to save the night's sleep for both of them. She is the one with agency, who can act while Morris can only fret. Morris is also taught an important lesson about ridding oneself of anxiety. It is worth noting that a psychiatrist friend, Owen Renick, first told this joke to me and prefaced it by telling me he would on occasion use it as a teaching tool with patients.

It sometimes seems to me that jokes with lessons in them are either about relationships between Jews and books (scholarship and learning) or Jews and money. Public radio's Ira Glass of *This American Life* once told me that Jews can be divided into "book Jews" and "money Jews." Certain Jews Ira might call "money Jews" surely look at book Jews, like Morris Goldfarb, who are barely able to eke out a living, as schlemiels. That is how my wife's businessman uncle looked at me. But before I go into that, let me offer a joke about book Jews and money Jews set in Israel, where a visitor attends a recital and concert at the Moskowitz Auditorium. He is impressed with the architecture and the acoustics. He inquires of the tour guide, "Is this magnificent auditorium named after Chaim Moskowitz, the famous Talmudic scholar?"

"No," replies the guide. "It is named after Sam Moskowitz, the writer."

"Never heard of him," says the visitor. "What did he write?"

"A check," says the guide.

Money Jews, who earn grand sums outside the professions, often have the good fortune of being blessed with what I call a financial *saichel*, the Yiddish word meaning common sense, but a word most often applied to a special kind of intelligence about money or business. I remember, as a kid, reading Stephen Birmingham's book *Our Crowd*, about the superwealthy New York banking Jews who lit cigars with hundred-dollar bills. Who, I wondered, were these Jews? Why wasn't I one of them? I was always a book Jew. Jews of an older generation than mine, even the off-the-scale moneymaking Jews, generally showed a modicum of respect for learning and erudition. But my then fiancée, now my wife, had an uncle who, other than loving opera, was a full-fledged money Jew. While I was at work on my Ph.D. in literature, he would frequently lecture, even hector, me on how I needed to stop being a schlemiel and wise up to making a more substantial income than I would as a scholar and professor—-especially since he knew his niece and I were planning to marry and eventually have a family. He once turned to me in the middle of a dinner with his wife and the girl I was soon to wed, and exclaimed, apropos of nothing, "Why do you want to be a *melamed* [teacher]? WHY DON'T YOU BECOME A REAL DOCTOR?"

When I taught Michael Gold's proletarian novel *Jews Without Money*, one of my black students, who would later become both a friend and a successful playwright, howled with laughter at the title. "There ain't no Jews without money," he exclaimed. I said to him: "You're looking at one," and then I went on to say how, yes, Jews had a piece of the American pie but there were still many, a surprising number, who were destitute. His response: "THEY GOT A MIGHTY BIG PIECE OF THAT PIE."

Trust me. There are plenty of Jews still with neither books nor much, if any, money. They are often called schlemiels.

> Two Jews stand in front of a firing squad are asked if they have a last wish. One says to the other, "How about if I ask for a cigarette?" The Jew next to him says, "Shush. Do you want to get us in trouble?"

The joke, probably right out of the shtetl, is also a schlemiel joke because meek Jews were often regarded as schlemiels. Even those Jewish characters who constantly badger and beg for money or goods, characters known as schnorrers, are not schlemiels because they can show moxie and assert themselves. But the fearful Jew, the Jew terrified of his own shadow, is as often as not relegated to schlemiel status.

Jewish humor can be scalding and aggressive or as astonishingly meek as the prototypical shtetl character Bontche Schveig (Bontche the Silent). A creation of the Polish Yiddish author I. L. Peretz, Bontche may be the ultimate passive schlemiel of all time since: whether out of fear or temperament, he does nothing to offend or displease anyone. In fact, he makes no mark at all in his journey through life, and is rapturously welcomed into heaven by Abraham and the angels for living a life of utter silence, anonymity, suffering, and loneliness. Never was there a cry or even a word of protest from poor Bontche while he was among the living, and as a result, he gets his final reward. He enters paradise with great fanfare for having lived a life so self-effacing that no one ever noticed his existence. With glittering jewels and a golden throne set for him to sit on, Bontche is put through a pro forma heavenly court trial. The prosecutor can offer nothing to say against him. Bontche is then told he can have whatever he wants. But all the meek Bontche can ask for, timorously, is a breakfast bun with butter. The prosecutor lets out a bitter laugh at the mordant humor of Bontche's incredible wish. Silence may be golden and the way to paradise for Bontche, but in reality, he is a pathetic schlemiel; if he were to drop his buttered bread on the ground, he would no doubt see it land on the buttered side. The real point of the story is that the lowly schlemiel can be blessed with heavenly fanfare and paradise. This would never be the case for a schmuck.

An extraordinarily wealthy man is approached by a leader from the Jewish community's welfare federation who seeks a donation. The solicitor brings to this Jewish moneybags's attention that he has never donated so much as a dime. The rich Jew responds with a touching lament about his mother and father's poverty and physical handicaps, and then says the same of his children and siblings. He concludes with: "If I won't give any of them a cent, why do you think I would give any money to you?"

Those who know their New Testament may recall how it is easier for a camel to go through the eye of a needle than it is for a rich man to enter the kingdom of heaven. What does that have to do with Jews, you well might ask, since it is from the *New* Testament?

One of the cornerstones of Jewish values has always been *tzedakah*, or acts of charity, even from those who can ill afford to be charitable. Charity, for Jews, has for centuries been both a religious and a moral obligation. The earth's fate depends on it, as we see in the religious (and folkloric) stories of the Lamed Vovnik, the thirty-six righteous Jews whose good deeds hold the fate of the earth in the balance.

Giving to strangers, the poor, or the disabled is also linked to *rachmones,* which roughly means compassion or a heart that pities others. But others can, of course, trip up even the best-intentioned mitzvah maker, as in the joke about the man who holds out a tin cup to an older Jewish woman and jangles the coins in it. Feeling pity for his apparent blindness, she reaches into her purse, removes every coin in it, and puts them all into the beggar's cup. He thanks her, and as she walks away, he says: "I knew you were kind the second I laid eyes on you."

The bogus beggar in that joke, like the rich man who refuses to give any money to Jewish charity, or even anyone in his immediate family, is a schmuck. And schmucks don't have to be Jewish. The brilliant (a word I try to use sparingly) Steve Jobs was someone I liked. He used to say when he saw me, as he did on a couple of occasions when I visited Pixar, "You are supposed to be in my dashboard." Good line. But despite his billions, he was notoriously stingy. I even asked his biographer, Walter Isaacson, who supposedly ferreted out all the darker sides of Jobs's character—including how badly and mean he could behave toward employees or women—if he knew whether or not Jobs ever donated money to charity. I knew his wife, Laurene, supported a number of good causes. But what about Jobs? Maybe, I prodded Isaacson, he gave anonymously? Walter didn't know. No one, in fact, seemed to know, though a close friend of his assured me that Jobs never had given or would give a dime to any cause. Conclusion? Steve Jobs was a great man, but he also was a schmuck.

A Jewish man goes to see his rabbi. He begins by reminding the rabbi that his father died just three weeks before. The rabbi says, "I know. Your father was a wonderful man. Everyone loved and appreciated him. I was at his *shiva*."

"I know, Rabbi," the man says. "Thank you for coming."

"Of course," says the rabbi. "Did you need to talk to me about your loss?"

"Well, Rabbi, I need to tell you that my father left me millions."

"I know," said the rabbi. "He was a remarkably good and successful businessman and he wanted you and your family to be well provided for."

"I know, Rabbi. But what you don't know is that the week after my father died, my maternal uncle passed away and he, too, left me millions. Then, just last week, my first cousin Bernie died of liver cancer and he also willed me millions of dollars."

"Well," said the rabbi, "all of those losses are terrible. You have my deepest condolences. I know how sad you must be. You are obviously understandably depressed. But all that money left to you shows how much your family members loved you and there is so much good you can do with the money."

"No, Rabbi. You don't understand. I'm depressed because, so far this week, NOTHING!"

Even a joke about a Jewish villain or a greedy Jewish schmuck will highlight the character's distinctiveness, as in many of the jokes about schmucks. You may not have to be Jewish (like the old Levy's bread ad said about loving their product) to be a schmuck, but if Jews are ruthless, villainous, cheap, or greedy, they are going to stand out. Think, for a moment, of the insatiable schmuck who obviously cannot be happy with any amount of money, and compare him to the schlemiel, who may also be unhappy but not out of a hunger for money or anything else in life. Schlemiels, for all their faults and mishaps, tend to be portrayed as resigned to what life metes out to them, often accepting their fate and failures as they stumble through.

I was visiting my elderly father at Menorah Park, a Jewish home for the aged in Cleveland, and a couple of old Jews were watching the television show *American Greed,* which profiles thieves, scoundrels, and con men. One of the older fellows said to a man sitting next to him, "Why are a lot of the schmucks on this show Jews?" He went on, philosophically, to tick off an impressive list of Jewish humanitarians and Jews of lofty achievement, and then, raising his voice, added, "Why do we have to see Jewish schmucks?"

Pride among Jews in fellow Jews who are schmucks? No. More mortification and, yes, too, concern over what the goyim might think.

A wife is furious at her husband and finally, after many years of a tumultuous and discord-filled marriage, she explodes, telling him she is leaving him and calling him a schmuck. "You were a schmuck when we first met and you've been a schmuck to me our entire married life. You are the second-biggest schmuck on the planet!"

The husband logically asks, "If I am such a schmuck, why am I only the second-biggest schmuck?"

His wife screams at him, "Because you're a schmuck!"

This is one of those jokes that is meant to be told rather than read, but its meaning is clear and it reveals how loaded and powerful the word "schmuck" can be. The wife is so exasperated at her husband for being a schmuck to her for so long that she won't allow him the consolation of being the worst schmuck of all schmucks.

The joke, more than most, reveals the power of a single word, "schmuck," when spoken aloud. A large part of Jackie Mason's shtick was in his delivery. A former rabbi, Mason was funny in large part because of the inflections and tone of voice he deployed. When I interviewed him on the air, I began by saying how impressed I was with his timing, and I added that I assumed he must have had to work as hard as any actor at perfecting it. His response, in the voice many love to imitate but few can replicate, was, "This is the stupidest thing anyone has ever said to me. That you should think a man of my great comic gifts and genius should have to work as hard as an actor to do what I do without a single flaw." That line was delivered with the sarcasm and mockery of pretension that had become the successful hallmark of Mason's humor. When the interview ended, I thanked Mason and told him I was grateful for having had him on the air. Here, again, he responded with his customary tone, saying, "Of course you're grateful. You got to be with me for an hour. It didn't cost you a cent."

Jackie Mason could use his voice like an instrument in order to be funny. He could make good jokes great just in the telling.

A Jewish man, who has been happily married for over fifty years, is alone for the first time after his wife is called away to help sort out her recently deceased sister's estate. His adult son has known for many years that his father would love to have a beautiful young sexual partner give him sex at least one time before he passes on. Whenever the father would see a lovely, shapely young woman on television or in a film, he would sigh and say, in Yiddish, "A *maidel mit vara!*" Which, translated, means, "A girl with the goods."

The son well understood and empathized with his father's yearnings and attractions to younger women, especially since it was clear to him that his mother had put way too much weight on and was covered with the road maps of varicose veins and the flabbiness, drooping, and wrinkles of age. So the son took it upon himself to send a young nubile beauty, a hooker, to his father, the aging Jew, for the thrill of a lifetime.

The father is home alone and the doorbell rings. A scantily clad beauty with a figure many women would kill for ardently grabs hold of him, kissing him wildly, and saying, repeatedly, "I am yours!" He is excited beyond measure.

The two head, hand in hand, right to the bedroom. This is exactly what the old Jew had imagined, dreamed of. "Soon," he thinks, "I will be *schtupping* this unbelievably gorgeous young woman, a dream come true."

Except he cannot perform. He is saddened and apologetic, but there, clearly, is nothing to be done. He sends the young beauty off and simply resigns himself to having flopped.

Two days later, his wife returns. She goes into the bedroom, the same one he could not perform in, to change her clothes, and he looks at her as she undresses and realizes he is fully aroused. He stares at his erection and, in spite of himself, blurts out: "SCHMUCK! NOW I KNOW WHY THEY CALL YOU A SCHMUCK!"

This joke is actually rather sweet. In spite of the father's wish to cheat on his wife, and despite the ravages of time, he is faithful to her and cannot rise to the occasion with the prostitute. But he is also angry and uses the word "schmuck" to let his own schmuck (his penis) know how angry he is at its inability to perform. As the old saying goes, a hard-on may have no conscience, but in this joke a flaccid penis apparently does.

The founder and owner of Goldberg's nail company decides, for the first time in his life, to go on a vacation. He heads to Miami Beach. He entrusts the running of his beloved company to his trusted, long-time assistant, Finkelstein, and his son Mark, a recent MBA graduate from Harvard. After a couple of days away in Florida, Finkelstein calls him and tells him he must return home immediately. When he repeatedly asks why, Finkelstein simply and mysteriously says, "You will know as soon as you are back on the highway. This is an emergency and you must return." So the old man stoically travels back north and hours later is in a rented car heading back to his nail factory, gravely concerned and obviously uncertain about what this is all about. At this point, he sees, on the highway, a huge billboard with a graphic picture of Jesus Christ on the cross and the unmistakable caption THEY USED GOLDBERG'S NAILS.

The old man is horrified. He is beside himself. Years of working to create good public relations with the community he established for his company seem annihilated and he knows this must be the handiwork of his Harvard MBA son. He is distraught. By the time he makes it to the factory, he is also incensed, and when he sees his son, he rips into him with fury. "How could you be so stupid? Where was your judgment? This is what I paid for you to go to Harvard to learn about running a business? You've set us back so badly we may never recover. How could you do this to me? To us?"

The son swears he will make it up and do right by his father and the company, and claims he knows exactly what to do. "Don't worry, Dad," the son says. But his father goes off cursing and brooding, wondering how they can repair the damage. The billboard comes down. But the next day a new billboard goes up. On it is the cross with Jesus in a hunched, fetal position. Beneath the cross and right below it is the caption THEY DIDN'T USE GOLDBERG'S NAILS.

This, of course, is a generational joke. It is also a joke about a son who is a schmuck and who, despite an expensive Ivy

League education, has no *saichel*. (Saul Bellow's son Gregory claimed that when he was a child, his famous Nobel laureate father told him to point to his behind and then to his elbow and then said to him, "Now you know as much as a Harvard graduate.") It is, too, a joke that shows the comfort level Jews have in America, suggested by the son who is not in the least perturbed about using Christ to sell his family's manufactured wares.

Let us conclude with the tale of a young Jew who is obsessed about the dearth of compassion in the world. He broods to the point where he finally is convinced by his parents to consult with the rabbi. Even though the rabbi has always seemed pompous and autocratic to the boy, "a real schmuck," as many of the boy's fellow Hebrew school pupils describe him, the lad makes an appointment and goes to see him. The rabbi's peremptory, brusque manner puts the boy off, but he ventures forth and says, "Rabbi. I want to understand. Why are so many people so apathetic and uncaring?" The schmuck rabbi looks directly at the kid and says, "I don't know and I don't care."

"A GOYISHE KOP!"

Yiddish,
Generations
&
Assimilation

It is the Depression. An older married Jewish couple are barely getting by. They see a sign in a store window that says WE CONVERT JEWS. ONE HUNDRED DOLLARS CASH. They agonize. They are hungry and poor. Doesn't the Talmud teach us, they reason, that we, made in God's image, must first and above all else care for ourselves? They decide, with trepidation and uncertainty, to go into the store and be converted, and following a baptismal immersion, Christian prayers, and signs of the cross, they are welcomed as converts into the religion of Jesus. The next morning the man wakes up, and as he has done his entire life, he begins to put on tefillin, the ritual phylacteries wound around the arms and placed on the forehead by pious, observant Jews. His wife sees him doing this and says, "What are you doing? Don't you remember? We are Christians now." Whereupon the man slaps his forehead and groans, "Oy! Already I have a *goyishe kop*!"

A grandfather takes his grandson for a walk. They stop in front of a small lake with a big sign saying NO SWIM-MING ALLOWED in large block letters. Below these words, the warning is repeated in even larger letters, with exclamation marks. The grandfather takes his grandson's hand and says, "Come on. Vee going to go for a svim." The grandson is incredulous. "But, Grandpa," he says, "it says no swimming allowed. It says it twice." The grandfather replies: "No. It says. No swimming allowed? No! Swimming allowed!"

T

HE JOKE about the couple who convert is rich in Jewish chauvinism, as so many modern Jewish jokes are, and serves to put Jews in a category separate from Gentiles. Neither obtuse nor forgetful, as the words *goyishe kop* imply, Jews are smart and blessed with Yiddish *kops* (brains). The important motif to note in the joke is that even with assimilation through conversion, some essence of Jewishness is retained.

Goyishe kop gives the joke its concluding comic lift—ideally recited with gusto and, at conclusion, a good slap to the forehead. The Yiddish words serve to connect Jews to the past and to their identity, while also suggesting that Jews do not easily give up their Jewish identity.

Without knowing or understanding Yiddish, the convert

joke, as well as the "No! Swimming Allowed!" joke, can be lost on the person hearing or reading it. With little if any grasp of the connotative power of Yiddish words and phrases, many jokes have a short shelf life. As an example, I think of my grandparents coming over in steerage from Russia, unwilling to allow anything unkosher to pass their lips, while my own children have gone on cruises and eaten shellfish, pork, and ham. How, I am often asked, can younger grandchildren and great-grandchildren ever understand the meaning of many of the older Jewish jokes, tales, or folklore, when they have never learned any Yiddish? How can they understand when they have never entered into what the literary critic Irving Howe aptly called "the world of our fathers"? Or, please, our mothers!

It is even difficult for many of today's young Jews to realize that their parents or grandparents lived during a period of exclusive clubs that would not accept Jews as members. Not even to mention college quotas. My father could not get into medical school because of strict quotas. I could not be a member of nearly all of the non-Jewish fraternities on the campus of my southern Ohio alma mater. That was simply how things were, and for the most part, there was acceptance if not acquiescence. But even when Jews couldn't all study at the top institutions or become doctors or lawyers because of quotas, there was, and still remains, rich, vibrant humor about Jewish distinctiveness. We see this in Groucho Marx's famous quip after being told he would be admitted to an exclusive Gentile club only if he didn't swim in the club's pool. Groucho (who also once famously said he would not want to join any club that wanted him as a member) was said to have asked if his daughter, who was half-Jewish, could wade in the pool up to her knees.

When my younger daughter and her boyfriend went to see *Old Jews Telling Jokes* on Broadway, they were aware of being the only young couple in the audience. I'm sure younger people have attended that show, just as occasionally younger men and women have come to my presentations of Jewish comedy. But they are often brought along or urged to go by parents who want to expose them to the past for which they, the parents, are nostalgic. When older generations of Jews wax poetic either about the golden age of Jewish comedy—or, as a documentary film title heralds it, *When Jews Were Funny*—it suggests the onetime pervasiveness of Jewish comedians who had Jewish mind-sets and were not Jewish solely by DNA.

I once emceed *An Evening of Jewish Humor* that included a talented roster of comedy stand-ups including Steve Landesberg, Brad Garrett, Richard Lewis, and Rita Rudner. The only real Jewish link among them was their gene pool. Only yours truly, who opened the evening, and Robin Williams, who was not a Jew but came onstage at the end with manic spritzing as the surprise final performer, were summoning Yiddish words or deploying recognizable Jewish content.

I always liked Canadian-born comedian David Steinberg's line about his father never getting to see his dream of an all-Yiddish-speaking Canada come true. The essential paradox of Jewish identity is that, as it becomes increasingly secular, the jokes reflect a greater need to preserve its values.

> **A Tel Aviv mother speaks to her children exclusively in Yiddish despite her friends and neighbors scolding her to speak in Hebrew. "Why are you so stubborn?" a friend of hers asks in exasperation. "It will do them no good to learn Yiddish." "Perhaps," says the mother. "But I don't want them to forget that they are Jewish."**

Jewish cultural values are embedded in Yiddishkeit. Before the birth of Israel, Hebrew was only the language of prayer. But as the mother in the joke, set in the modern Hebrew-speaking city of Tel Aviv, is saying, Jewish identity is rooted in the mother tongue of Yiddish.

Consider a story told by Sam Levenson, a popular figure in television during the 1950s, in which a Jewish mother brags to her mahjongg group about her son spending so much time with his grandfather during summer vacation. "He even learned from his *zayde* how to count in Yiddish," she proudly says to the other ladies. Whereupon she summons her boychick and asks him to show the ladies how he can count in Yiddish. The boy proceeds: "*Eyns, tsvey, dray, fir, finef, zeks, zibn, akht, nayn, sven.* Jack. Queen. King. Ace."

The story has obvious charm. The grandson in it has formed an apparent bond with his *zayde* and has actually learned to count to ten in Yiddish. Though the context is card playing, a transgenerational joke like this is affirming.

The joke about the grandfather who takes his grandson for a walk and then proposes a swim also unites generations—with an implicit meaning of a passing on of the past. The Yiddish grandfather provides his own interpretation of the prohibition against swimming—which he renders with a lively Yiddish inflection and rhythm.

We see again what is evidenced in many Jewish jokes, a preserving of the past unto a later generation. The preserving is less in learning Yiddish numbers or Yiddish inflections and rhythms than it is in the relationship of grandfather and grandson and in the idea of learning being passed down. In the words of my friend the novelist and pioneering psychiatrist

Irwin Yalom, "We're passing on something of ourselves . . . that's what makes our life full of meaning."

Most of the roots of Jewish humor we have come to know and love not only emerged from the Ashkenazi Jewish experience, but also became linked to other nations where Jews lived and thrived. Perhaps, as the novelist Saul Bellow once said, in discussing how Jewish and Irish humor are alike, "Oppressed people tend to be witty." But Jews have not been oppressed for some time now in most Western countries. They've been discriminated against, disdained, and even despised, but not—as in the painful past of history—oppressed, tortured, or killed by government fiat for the crime of being Jewish. Still, many Jews remain painfully aware of the past, even continuing to feel marginalized or victims of anti-Semitism. This has become true in our own time with much wrath directed against Israel. But even that can be turned into a joke spanning generations, as in the one about the great-grandfather in Israel who points to a tree and says to his great-grandson, "I planted that tree." Then he points to a house and tells his great-grandson, "I built that house." The great-grandson asks, "Great-grandpa, were you an Arab?"

Or take the joke about the Jewish father in the twenty-first century who is walking with his son when he is stopped by a passerby who tells him how handsome the boy is. He proudly thanks the stranger, who then proceeds to ask the boy's name. "Shlomo," the father replies. "Shlomo?" says the passerby. "What kind of name is Shlomo?" The father answers: "He's named after his dead grandfather whose name was Scott."

I love that joke. It has within it the seeds of hope for a renaissance in Jewish tradition in generations to come. Most Jews continue to name their children after the dead and often use the first letter of the name of a deceased loved one with a more assimilated name (like Scott). The man's son in the joke is given an *S* name right out of Yiddishkeit, a name far away from the contemporary.

What is especially archetypal about Jewish humor is the tie it almost always has to differentness, separateness, chosenness, and loss. Yiddish can embody all of that. Consider Jon Stewart's hilarious bit "Faith Off," in which he claimed to be getting personal, focusing on Passover versus Easter. He dramatically entreats his fellow Jews, calling them *mishpocheh*, the Yiddish word for family or extended family, and pleads with them to bring Passover up a notch for the sake of keeping Jewish children Jewish, including his own half-Jewish kids. Stewart takes out an Easter basket and points to the chocolate and bunnies in it, asking his fellow Jewish parents how they can possibly compete—comparing a basket of goodies and bunny rabbits to a traditional Passover plate, replete with horseradish and a bone from a dead baby lamb.

Jewish youth of today need more than a transfusion of Yiddish to claim their Jewishness and heritage. In what could easily be seen as an assimilation joke, my brother Victor tells a tale of working at the San Francisco Jewish Community Center when a young Jewish member, reading an announcement that the center would be closed on the two Jewish holidays of Succoth and Shavuot, asked him: "What does closing the center have to do with suck it and shove it?"

Jewish jokes often reveal loss of faith or lack of understanding of Judaism itself, as in the joke about the young Jew who goes to see an Orthodox rabbi to ask for a *barucha,* or blessing, to be said by the rabbi over his new Mercedes. The Orthodox rabbi is outraged and says he has no wish to say a *barucha* over a German car and tells the young car owner to go to the Conservative rabbi down the block. The young Jew goes to the Conservative rabbi and asks for a *barucha* only to be told by that rabbi that he knows no *baruchas* for cars. Perhaps, he advises, the young man might want to see a Reform rabbi in a synagogue nearby. The young man finds the Reform rabbi and asks him if he can say a *barucha* over his new Mercedes. The Reform rabbi informs the young man that he, too, has a Mercedes, and asks what model of Mercedes and how many miles it can get to the gallon. Then the reform rabbi asks: "What is a *barucha*?"

The joke is also told featuring a young Jew seeking a mezuzah for his Ferrari. The Reform rabbi asks, "What's a mezuzah?"

In either form, the joke is really about the anxiety over the loss of Judaism's essential meaning as it becomes more secular—and about materialism supplanting traditional Jewish values. It demonstrates, too, how young Jews can misunderstand or misapply something as sacred as a *barucha*. And it alludes to the commonly held belief (also a Jewish joke itself) that the three branches of Judaism can never agree, with the Reform movement appearing especially adrift from traditional Jewish practice.

Three modern rabbis are arguing about which of the three is the most progressive.

"I am definitely the most progressive," says the first rabbi. "We allow smoking during services."

"That's nothing," replies the second rabbi. "We serve pork spareribs during Yom Kippur."

"Not bad," replies the third rabbi. "But I have you all beat. During Rosh Hashanah and Yom Kippur, we post signs at my temple—CLOSED FOR THE HOLIDAYS."

Jewish comics have drawn from their own lives to highlight assimilation humor. Woody Allen once spoke of his rabbi being so Reformed he was a Nazi. Jackie Mason, too, did a riff on a Jew refusing to buy a Mercedes because it is a German car. Mason joked that other German-made goods, especially if offered at bargain prices, seemed to get a pass. The stand-up comic London Lee, née Alan Levine, once said he had a German shepherd as a pet until it found out he was Jewish and bit him.

But the *barucha* joke may also be yet another kind of crowing over Jewish prosperity. It simultaneously draws our attention to the success of Jews who can actually afford a Mercedes or a Ferrari, while harshly criticizing, through humor, how much Jews, especially young Jews and Reform rabbis, have migrated from Judaism to materialism.

Material success can, indeed, be the measure of success for refugees. It can, too, even include anti-Semitism. As in the joke about the two Jewish refugees who make their way to America and vow to meet at the same place in a year. They make a bet over who will do better materially and who will become the more assimilated. They meet. The first Jew says, "I made my first hundred thousand dollars and my wife is in the PTA. My kid is in Little League. We eat regularly at McDonald's and barbecue every weekend. What about you?"

The second Jew gives him a cold stare and says, "Fuck you, Jewboy."

It is illuminating to note that I heard the same joke, years later, with the refugees being Muslims from an Arab country and the one calling the other a camel jockey.

A wide range of Jewish jokes about the loss of Jewish identity are also about what Nietzsche called "eternal return" and what we might call the shadow of the past. When the black entertainer and Rat Pack member Sammy Davis Jr. converted to Judaism, a joke went around that Sammy tried to get on a bus in the Jim Crow South and was ordered by the bus driver to get to the back of the bus. "But I'm Jewish," Sammy pleaded. Whereupon the bus driver said, "Get off the bus."

That joke was especially popular when Jews were in vogue in America and "philo-Semitism" (the opposite of anti-Semitism) was at its summit. Not only Sammy Davis, but a number of other Hollywood icons, including Marilyn Monroe and Elizabeth Taylor, converted to Judaism. (Lenny Bruce got big laughs on Steve Allen's old television show simply by announcing that he would attend Elizabeth Taylor's bat mitzvah.) At heart, both the joke about the *barucha*-seeking Mercedes or Ferrari owner and the one about Sammy Davis on a segregated bus in the South are variations on the same theme: anxiety about being Jewish.

A couple of landsmen, fellow Jews, see a sign offering a hundred dollars to any Jew who will convert. One of the two Jews, Murray, decides to investigate and asks his friend, Harry, to wait for him. Murray is gone a long time, and when he finally returns, Harry asks, "Well. Did you get the money?" Murray says, "Why is that the first thing you people think about?"

In this joke, there is anxiety over loss of Jewish identity. Many Jewish jokes, such as the one about the conversion and the *goyishe kop*, are about this fear, and about the need to relinquish Jewish identity in order to make it financially. This was especially true in harsher times, like the Depression, when there were actual quotas and formidable barriers standing in the way of Jews making progress. The great German writer Heinrich Heine converted from Judaism to Christianity and called his conversion a passport to acceptance. Many Jews in the United States felt the need to change their Jewish-sounding last names in order to advance or gain acceptance. Even Jews who retained names like Shapiro, Levine, or Katz gave their names more English-sounding pronunciations. Of course there were many permutations of Jewish-sounding names as years went by. Ralph Lifshitz, for example, became Ralph Lauren. Jonathan Leibowitz and Lorne Lipowitz became Jon Stewart and Lorne Michaels. According to my friend Phil Bronstein, his father knew a man named Green who came from Europe and decided he wanted an American-sounding name. He changed his to Greenberg. Now, that's funny! Jewish jokes are often about some vestige of Jewishness that cannot be covered up, discarded, or lost.

A couple try for years to get entrance into an all-WASP country club that will not accept Jews as members. Finally, Morris and Rose gain membership in the club because Morris, or Moishe, as he is known to his Jewish friends, agrees to donate a couple million to a capital campaign, which will mean a whole new building for the previously restrictive club. Now that they are members, Rose is eager and excited to be there and she dresses up for a grand entrance to the evening's dinner for all club members. Rose appears with a full-length mink coat and her finest and most expensive, gaudy jewelry. Upon entering, she immediately sees modestly and underdressed women with only the most tasteful and not at all conspicuous or flashy jewelry. She realizes how out of whack her appearance is compared to these WASP women and she cannot suppress the single word that escapes her mouth. Loudly and audible to all around her the word tumbles out. *"GEVALT,"* the Yiddish word that is an exclamation of shock or alarm. She looks swiftly around at the placid and aloof and modestly dressed WASP women and says, "Vatever dat means."

Do younger Jews understand the feeling of exclusion integral to such jokes, an exclusion once commonplace? If they are not familiar with their people's history, extending back a couple of generations, these kinds of jokes can fall flat. They need only talk to older Jews in their family or watch a film like *Gentleman's Agreement,* a 1947 movie in which Gregory Peck plays a reporter posing as a Jew and encounters widespread anti-Semitism.

The comedian Jack Carter once said his favorite Jewish joke was the one that takes us back to the era of Barry Goldwater. Goldwater was the in-your-heart-you-know-he's-right conservative Republican from Arizona who ran for president against Lyndon Baines Johnson. He was scion of a well-to-do, once-Jewish family whose name was originally Goldwasser.

A man named Schwartz calls up a man named Goldwater and complains to him. "How come, Goldwater,

I can't get in the club and you got in?" Goldwater responds: "Mr. Schwartz. My name is Goldwater. It is not Goldwasser. It is not Goldvasser. I am an Episcopalian. My father is an Episcopalian. My grandfather, *alav ha-shalom,* he was an Episcopalian."

Even in the face of conversion or assimilation, the customary Yiddish (and Hebrew) words for the dead, *alav ha-shalom,* are uttered.

Both the Goldwater joke and the *gevalt* joke are really about Jewish identity seemingly lost yet in some form remaining. Schwartz may not get into the club, but Goldwater may not really belong either, despite being a member. The *gevalt* lady, Rose, and her husband, Moishe, finally make it into the restricted club through Moishe's extravagant donation, but, again, the manner in which she dresses up and the one single Yiddish word she utters set her apart. Both jokes seem to say that Jews retain distinctiveness, even if they social-climb to become Gentile club members. Traces of Yiddish, which humorously expose the bloodline, remain. They never truly can be goyim!

Much of the Jewish past and Jewish identity has, of course, become eroded by time and assimilation. Identity somehow remains, however—as in the story of the Jew who converts to

Catholicism and becomes a priest. He presents his first sermon in a cathedral to a large number of devout Catholics. He begins the sermon with: "My fellow goyim."

I recall feeling a small sense of exclusion myself one evening, when, as a young professor, I attended the birthday party of a Gentile friend at his private and swanky club with no other Jews in sight. The friend who invited me was a Harvard WASP, and I was seated with friends of his, all young WASP types who were comparing notes on where they lived when they were at Harvard. "Weren't you in Quincy House?" one of them asked. "No, I was in Mather House." "Oh," said a third, "I was supposed to be in Mather House but I wound up at Adams." And so it went. Until, as if realizing the need to be civil, one of them finally turned to me and asked, "You weren't at Harvard, were you?" I said, deadpan, "No. I was in Hillel House at Ohio University."

I'm not even sure they knew what Hillel House was (a Jewish campus organization). But I deliberately chose those wry words. My feelings of exclusion may have had as much to do with class as with being the lone Jew in a clique of WASPs.

A young Jewish man escapes the Holocaust and makes his way to England, where he manages,

through sheer entrepreneurial genius, to make a fortune. His old widower father remains behind in the Warsaw ghetto and the young man is able to pay for an incredible, daring, and expensive airlift to rescue him. Once his father is safe in England, the young man tells him he must think of himself as an Englishman. "That is what I am now, Papa," he explains to the old man. "This land has given me refuge and a haven and I have succeeded here. I am, by God, an Englishman and you must think of yourself as one from now on, too."

He takes his father to Bond Street and has him fitted for and dressed in a brand-new expensive suit in a haberdashery there. Then he takes him to a fancy tonsorial place where the old man is put in the barber chair and the hair cutter begins cutting the old man's *payos,* the locks of hair worn by religious Hasidim. The father is suddenly sobbing convulsively and his son, with deep compassion as he watches his father's hair locks tumble to the floor, sympathetically asks: "What, Papa? Are you crying because you feel you are losing your Jewish identity?" The old man shakes his head, sniffs, and, with another convulsive sob, says: "No, son. I'm crying because we lost India."

In 2005, I told that joke on the air to the Indian author Vikram Seth when we discussed *Two Lives*, the memoir he wrote about the marriage of his England-based uncle to a Holocaust survivor. I also told it off the air to Salman Rushdie, who was born in India and then lived in England. Both Seth and Rushdie seemed to relish the joke and so do I. It is clearly an assimilation joke but one rendered by a cultural contrast that humorously, and painfully, shows how fast assimilation can take place for Jews, especially in the wake of something as catastrophic as the Shoah. Yet there is also a recognition of an ability Jews have possessed over centuries to adapt to and even embrace other cultures—especially those that provide opportunities to succeed without being discriminated against, put into a ghetto, or murdered.

I taught a course in the 1970s on Jewish writers. A leading minister of a major local church attended all of the classes. In the last class he surprised all of us by announcing that he had been born in Holland, raised a Jew, and, along with his entire family, converted to Christianity following their escape from the Nazis. When I asked what drew him to take a class in Jewish authors, he smiled and said, "I kind of got tired of being around all those goyim."

> Mice are running rampant all over the synagogue. Women are frightened, children are racing for cover, and the men have no notion what to do.
>
> "Don't worry," the rabbi announces. "I'll take care of it."
>
> The next day the mice are gone. The people in the synagogue are amazed! Finally, an older man stands up in the middle of a service and asks, "Rabbi, how did you do it? How did you get rid of all those mice?"
>
> "Easy," the Rabbi answers. "I bar mitzvahed them. And as everyone knows, once they're bar mitzvahed, they never come back."

Creating humor out of Jews leaving their religion is yet another way of lamenting assimilation and the escape from a Jewish life, in this case one anchored in the shul (temple or synagogue). Truth be told, many young Jewish boys, especially if they are from a Reform or secular-leaning family background, scurry off from religious involvement once they have a bar mitzvah, the party, and have been showered with money and gifts. I inevitably think of the joke about the boy on the day of his bar mitzvah who is told he is now a man and will be connected from that day forward, for the rest of his life, to all previous generations. The kid responds: "Today I am a man. Tomorrow I return to the seventh grade."

I heard the joke about the rabbi getting rid of the synagogue's mice many years ago, and I saw it retold by Marlo Thomas in a tribute she wrote following the death of Sid Caesar, the great Jewish comedian of *Your Show of Shows*. It was, she said, a favorite joke of Caesar's. Thomas is the daughter of Danny Thomas, a Lebanese American comedian who, like Garry Marshall of *Happy Days* fame, was constantly mistaken for a Jew.

I need briefly to get off the main topic because Marlo Thomas reminds me of a story I tell that has nothing to do with Jews or Jews and generations or Jews and assimilation or Yiddish, all of which I will get back to. The story, told to me by the award-winning fiction writer Tobias Wolff at an annual authors and ideas festival in Pebble Beach, was about Ronald Reagan, when he was president of the United States. President Reagan was getting a briefing by the Lebanese ambassador to the U.S. Those in attendance could not get over how attentive he was as the ambassador went into details with a set of maps showing the difficult geopolitical turmoil Lebanon was facing.

They all claimed they had rarely seen President Reagan look so rapt and intense. When the ambassador's briefing ended, Reagan went running up to him exclaiming, "Do you have any idea how much you look like Danny Thomas?"

An old Jewish man is about to testify in a courtroom trial and the examining attorney asks him to state his name for the court. He answers: "Isadore Rubin." Then the attorney asks him to state his age. "*Kenahora.* I'm ninety-three," says Mr. Rubin. The judge says to the attorney, "Please tell Mr. Rubin simply to state his age." He asks the lawyer to redirect and the lawyer obligingly asks, "Mr. Rubin. Would you kindly state your age for the court?" Mr. Rubin responds: "*Kenahora.* I'm ninety-three." The judge is immediate in his response, saying, "Mr, Rubin. You must simply answer the question directly and not add anything. If you do so again, I will be compelled to find you in contempt." A young Jewish lawyer who is seated in the courtroom and has been observing all this, suddenly, boldly comes forward and faces the judge. "Your Honor," he begins. "I believe, if you will permit me, I can solve this problem if you will allow me to question the witness." The judge looks at the young man with skepticism, but says, "This is highly unorthodox but I will allow it." Whereupon the young Jew turns to the old Jew and says: "Mr. Rubin. *Kenahora!* How old are you?"

This famous story, a version of which is told by Leo Rosten in *The Joys of Yiddish,* is really about the use of the Yiddish word *kenahora,* a word traditionally used to ward off evil, such as the father or mother of a newborn saying, "We have, *kenahora,* a beautiful, healthy baby."

Think, too, of the great stand-up comic Myron Cohen telling the joke about an older Jewish man in Miami who suffers a heart attack right on Collins Avenue and is helped to a stretcher by a young Jewish physician, who puts a pillow under the elderly man's head and asks: "Are you comfortable?" The old Jew responds, with a Yiddish inflection, "I make a living."

That joke, too, has its obvious charm. Aside from showing how financial status takes precedence in the old man's view of the world, the joke links an old Jew and his Yiddish idiom to a young Jew who is there to assist and care for him. It is no accident that Myron Cohen's joke and the *kenahora* joke feature a doctor and a lawyer as members of a younger generation of Jews coming to the assistance of older Jews.

> An elderly lady on a plane gets up from her seat and asks a young male passenger in a seat farther up in the plane if he is Jewish. "No, ma'am," he responds, and she goes back to her seat, only to return a few minutes later and ask the same stranger again if he is Jewish. Once more, he tells her he is not and she returns to her seat. When she gets up a third time and asks him, he shrugs his shoulders in frustration, looks to those seated next to him as if to say "what the hell," and says to her, "Yes. Yes, I am." The old lady says: "Funny. You don't look it."

My mother, Betty Krasny, loved telling that joke. It has a quaintness to it that seems to be connected to her generation and yet it still holds up like fine wine.

And speaking of fine wine, did you hear about the merger of Manishevitz and Christian Brothers? They are calling the new company *Manishaygetz*. Only those younger generation-als who know the word *"shegetz"* means a Gentile male would be able to understand that joke without an explanation.

> Two men are arguing heatedly over how to pronounce the name of America's fiftieth state. One man says it's "Hawaii," the other insists "Havaii." They argue. They make a large wager. Then they see a long-bearded rabbinic-looking figure who seems like a sage, and one of the men points to him and says to the other, "Let's have him decide." They agree that the bet will be settled by the older man and they put the question to him. Hawaii or Havaii? The old man stares off contemplatively into the distance, tugs at his beard, and then quickly pronounces, "Havaii." The winner of the bet is ecstatic. He says, "Thank you!" The old man responds: "You're velcome."

Just a silly joke based on a Yiddish accent and pronunciation, right? Yes. Or so it might seem. A simple joke based on a Yiddish accent would be more like the one about the Jewish immigrant taking an oral exam in his English as a Second Language class who is asked to spell "cultivate," and spells it correctly. He is then asked to use the word in a sentence, and, with a big smile, responds: "Last vinter on a very cold day, I vas vaiting for a bus, but it was too cultivate, so I took the subway."

A rabbi, as was often customary in the world of the shtetl, listens as two men present to him their individual versions of a money dispute. As the two men relate their conflicting narratives, the rabbi's wife stands nearby, within earshot. When the first man is done with his side of the story, the rabbi exclaims, "You're right!" But then, after the second man concludes his side, the rabbi also exclaims, "You're right!" Overhearing all this, the rabbi's wife speaks up and says, "How can they both be right? They are in total disagreement." The rabbi turns to his wife and says, "You're right, too!"

Is the joke saying that the rabbi is a pushover, inclined simply to agree with whoever is presenting a specific point of view? Or is it simply funny because of the impossibility of all three being right? What I believe is really going on in this joke may be a lesson for all of us from a rabbi, who, remember, is first a teacher (the word "rabbi" itself means teacher). Embedded in the joke are centuries of rabbinical commentary on religious arguments, all included in the Midrash—or Jewish commentaries. Midrash, like the Thomas Aquinas question about how many angels can dance on the head of a pin, is essentially about interpretations of biblical text, also called hermeneutics. The first time I heard that word I was in a graduate seminar, and half-asleep from my prof's droning voice. I asked him to please repeat Herman's last name. The message of the joke, then, is the impossibility of truly interpreting Midrash, notwithstanding all of the tomes of rabbinic commentaries. No angels can dance on the head of a pin, or one can, or an infinite number can. Every answer is "right," so the joke, like the Hawaii/Havaii one, reveals the ambiguity of truth and connects us back to Jewish tradition. *Why does a Jew answer every question with another question? The answer (preferably voiced aggressively) is: Why shouldn't a Jew answer every question with another question?*

I learned Hebrew as a boy with Ashkenazi pronunciation and then had to switch to Sephardic when that became customary and accepted. Can we really say Sephardic pronunciation is correct, especially to those who continue to use Ashkenazi? The switch confused me as a kid. I asked the rabbi if God was as apt to hear prayers in Sephardic as he had been in Ashkenazi.

Many years after, I noticed that my father, in the Jewish home, was still saying prayers with Ashkenazi pronunciation. When I asked him why, since, like everyone else, he had been praying for years in Sephardic, he said, "You always remember to pray in the first language you learn." In those later years, he had also gone back regularly to reading the Bible. When I asked him why, he said he was studying for his final exams.

An older Jewish woman on a bus says to a younger woman, "If you knew what I had, you would give up your seat to me." The conscience-stricken younger woman does so and the older woman sits down as the bus rambles on until she gets up and says to the bus driver, "If you knew what I have, you would come to an immediate stop at the next intersection." Even though it is not a regular stop on his route, the bus driver, a compassionate man, defies the rules and brings the bus to a halt. As he opens the door for the woman and courteously walks her down the steps of the bus, he asks her, "Could you, please, tell me what it is you have?" Stepping down and leaving the bus, she loudly responds, "Chutzpah!"

"Chutzpah" means gall or brazenness—some used to say you couldn't really possess it if you didn't pronounce it right. The definition of "chutzpah"? A kid who kills both his parents and pleads to a judge for leniency because he is an orphan. This and other Yiddish-word-based jokes culminate in a single Yiddish-word punch line, as in the joke ending in *goyishe kop*. The Yiddish is what separates the woman from the other characters. The punch relies not only on the dramatic-sounding word but also on its manifold associations.

An old Jewish man, Teitlebaum, is on his deathbed. His entire family is with him at his side as he lies at death's door. He has lived the life, his entire adult life, of a *shayner* Yid, a beautiful Jew, a life of rectitude, trustworthiness, honor, and respect, never missing a Friday-night or a Saturday-morning service and praying, davening piously, every morning and evening. His family is bewildered and frankly horrified when he asks, as his dying wish, to go through a conversion to Christianity. He tells them to get a priest or a minister, it doesn't matter, he simply must be converted to the faith of Christ before he passes on.

Knowing him to be unwavering in his decisions and also wanting to honor his deathbed wish, the family finds a Christian reverend who performs a deathbed conversion. The reverend leaves. The family cannot believe what has occurred. "Why, Pop?" his oldest son asks. "Why, after being a religious Jew all of your life, did you want to convert?" The old man smiles faintly and says, with the last breaths of his life, "Better one of them than one of us."

Loyalty to one's Jewish identity is a strong and enduring Jewish value. What the joke is also telling us is that Teitlebaum's Jewish identity, even with conversion, cannot be altered. Jewish identity can be tenacious, inescapable (like the old joke about the Jew who tells his friend he has completely shed his Jewish identity, when the two see a man resembling Quasimodo and the friend says, "And that guy says he's not a hunchback"). Teitelbaum is a good Jew his entire life, and being a good Jew, in the end, means loyalty to the tribe.

Tribal (and I don't mean Navajo or Apache) loyalty was tied for over a millennium to *mamaloshen*, the Yiddish word for the mother tongue. It was the native language for most European Jews until the Holocaust.

Ephraim Kishon, one of Israel's great humorists, who escaped the firing squad in a concentration camp because of his ability to play chess, once described Israel as "the only place on earth where the people read English, write in Hebrew, and joke in Yiddish." The ranks of Yiddish speakers, or even those who understand Yiddish, have, of course, thinned to meager numbers—though many Yiddish words have become part of the English lexicon. Yet the values of the tribe remain even after the language has nearly disappeared.

I remember watching Woody Allen's *Love and Death* back in 1975, at a matinee in a small movie theater in the town of Novato, California. Few people were in the theater, and at one point, the character played by Woody takes the hand of a woman clearly cast for her less-than-fetching looks. He kisses it and tells her it is a pleasure to meet "the Countess Mieskeit." The Yiddish word for a homely woman, *mieskeit,* was one I hadn't heard in years. An admittedly sexist and politically incorrect word by today's standards, it caused me to laugh out loud and the few other matinee goers to look at me in bewilderment. Though they had no idea why I was laughing, I was experiencing, courtesy of Woody Allen, a communal memory.

Cultural, social, even political differences between Jews and Gentiles (an old adage about American Jews is they earn like Episcopalians and vote like Puerto Ricans) are satirized, but ultimately it is Yiddish, a language few young Jews now know or understand, that separates not only the Jew from the Gentile but generations of Jews from each other.

When my friend Michael Murphy, the cofounder of the Esalen Institute, went to Hollywood in 2009 to work on the script of the film based on his novel *Golf and the Kingdom*, he assured me that he was doing what he needed to do to make the movie a success—he was learning Yiddish. I told Michael that Yiddish is no longer the mother tongue in Hollywood. There are still a lot of Jews there, but most are too young to know much, if any, Yiddish.

A tough New York Jew is captured by cannibals. The cannibals take him into their village, where they also have, tied and bound, a Frenchman and a German. A cannibal leader in a loincloth steps forward and says to the trio, in fluent English, as he points to a huge boiling cauldron of vegetables, "Gentlemen, we are going to cook you in that giant pot you see over there and eat you. But before we do, we will strip off your skin and build a canoe from it. The canoe will be in our tribe for generations. But first, since I was educated in the West before returning to my tribe, I must tell you we are humane cannibals and under my leadership we will let each of you choose the manner in which you will die." Rapidly, the German, assuming they do not have a luger, asks to be shot by one. The chief cannibal sends one of his fellow natives to fetch a gun and they kill the German with it. Then the Frenchman, assuming they do not have a guillotine, asks for death by that device. The chief cannibal quickly lops off the Frenchman's head. Then it is the tough New York Jew's turn, and he asks, in a thick New York accent, for a fork. The head cannibal, puzzled, repeats, "A fork?" and the tough New York Jew says, again, "Yeah. A fork." Whereupon, surprisingly, the cannibal leader pulls a fork out from his loincloth and hands it to the tough New York Jew—who proceeds to stab himself deeply and repeatedly in the chest, angrily shouting, "HERE'S YOUR FUCKIN' CANOE."

Jews have moved away from the shtetl and Yiddish and all the images of weakness and passivity they associate with them, and this joke gives us a picture of the tough, fully assimilated New York Jew. The joke essentially recasts jokes showcasing meek, passive shtetl victims or uxorious husbands, and celebrates a stronger, more militant contemporary Jewish figure—

New York born and bred. The joke also, of course, shows that the tough New York Jew can also have the last word.

As Lenny Bruce said: you are "Jewish" if you are from New York. The toughness associated with New York is in the joke about the elderly lady who arrives from the Midwest and finds herself lost. She assumes she will be treated rudely and aggressively, so she conjures up her own inner New Yorker. She goes up to the first New Yorker she sees, and says, "Excuse me. I know I should go fuck myself, but I wonder if you would first kindly help me with directions."

Not all tough Jews hail from New York. I would be remiss if I did not take note of the fact that, despite all of the jokes portraying weakness and meekness and husbandly docility, there were plenty of tough Jews (and not only the mobsters I learned about in a book called *Tough Jews* by Rich Cohen). I was educated about the Jews who fought back during the Holocaust from Yuri Suhl's book *They Fought Back*. Later on, I read the amazing story of my friend Joseph Pell, who became one of the San Francisco Bay Area's most successful businessmen. As a kid, Joe escaped into the forest after his family was wiped out by the Nazis. He went on to fight with the partisans after the Germans invaded Poland; throughout the war, still just a boy, he blew up train tracks, bombed bridges, and took revenge against those who informed on his family to the Nazis.

Following Israel's victory in the Six-Day War, a class of students is undergoing instruction in a Russian War College in the then USSR. They are discussing how a war with China might be fought with an army of only two hundred million or so while the Chinese army would easily come close to a billion. The brightest student in the class asks the Soviet general in charge how they could possibly hope to win a war against so many Chinese. The general quickly points out to the student that Israel has just won a war with only two or three million soldiers, while their Arab adversaries had some hundred million. The student quickly responds: "Okay. But how are we going to get three million Jews?"

We can look to Israel, where toughness became the focus of a number of jokes, especially popular ones following the victory in the Six-Day War. With Israel, a new Jewish identity emerged, replacing images of weakness and passivity. Many jokes portray Israelis as tough and even invincible; others as rude and brusque.

With rudeness, too, comes a new type of Jew. Take the joke about the man with a clipboard who approaches an American, a Pole, a Russian, and an Israeli and says, "Excuse me, gentlemen, but I am taking a survey and I would like to know your opinion of the meat shortage." The Pole asks, "What's meat?" The Russian asks, "What's an opinion?" The American asks, "What's a shortage?" and the Israeli asks, "What's 'excuse me'?" Or the joke about the Israeli rowing team: one man rows while the others stand up in the boat yelling. Or the joke about the man who is flying on El Al, the Israeli airline, and is asked by the flight attendant if he wants dinner. He asks, "What are my choices?" The flight attendant says, "Yes or no."

A Jewish immigrant is at Ellis Island entering the United States. He has, among his belongings, four sets of false teeth. All the sets are made of gold and are being examined by an immigration officer. The officer informs the immigrant that he cannot bring in all the gold. There is simply too much. Whereupon the Jewish immigrant tells the officer in English that he is Orthodox and needs all four sets for dietary purposes. The immigration officer looks skeptical. "I know some things about Jews and kosher eating. Why would you need four sets of gold teeth?" The Jewish immigrant responds, "I am very Orthodox. Extremely pious. I use one set for milk products and one for meat and a third for breaking the fast on Yom Kippur, the holiest of all days on the Jewish calendar." "I see," says the immigration officer, now looking less skeptical. "You are obviously a very religious man. But you only mentioned three religious occasions. What is the fourth?" "Oh," the Jewish immigrant muses, "that's just for when I want a ham sandwich."

Why my father, Zaz Krasny, loved that joke, as well as others about religious Jews eating ham or pork, was in part that they point out the often hypocritical ways of the kashrut-enforcing Jews. That kind of joke carried a lot more power to a generation brought up observing or simply aware of the dietary laws than it does to the thousands of Jewish youth today who were raised on ham, pork, and shellfish. But it still holds up simply because most young Jews, even if totally secular, know ham is verboten to religious Jews and find humorous the obvious hypocrisy that the joke lampoons. According to Pew research, Orthodoxy continues to burgeon in America and elsewhere.

A lot of the Jewish jokes young people tell now are topical. A Jewish student of mine, knowing my love for Jewish jokes, came running up to me after Arnold Schwarzenegger was elected governor of California asking me if I knew what you got when you crossed Arnold with a Jew. The answer was Conan the Distributor. Those kinds of topical, silly jokes, even though amusing, often seem superficial, yet younger Jews, unaware of Jewish history and adversities, are often more attuned to them. There is both pride and humor in hearing Adam Sandler rattle off his amusing lines, like the one in his Hanukkah song about putting together half Jews Paul Newman and Goldie Hawn and "getting one fine-looking Jew." But most often such jokes lack a real, historical frame of reference.

Jewish jokes mostly tell us, as Scott Fitzgerald said about the rich, that Jews are different. As we get to a younger demographic, more removed from Old World Jewish values, differences are increasingly tied to stereotypes. Woody Allen took stereotypes of Jewish cheapness to another level in his line "I'm very proud of my gold pocket watch. My grandfather, on his deathbed, sold me this watch."

One can discern, in a host of Jewish jokes, anxiety about assimilation and loss of Jewish identity. But also, as we have seen, in these jokes there is pride in being different and superior, or in being well off and successful, in contrast to the penury of the past—especially the poverty of the shtetl. Is a lot of this humor not also defensive? No doubt.

I end with a true tale of assimilation about the daughter of my friend and colleague Eric Solomon who decided one day that she wanted to be more Jewish. Though both her parents were Jewish by birth, Madeline and her brother were raised without religious affiliation and the family had a Christmas tree in their home each year. So when Madeline announced at age fifteen that she was staying home from school because it was Yom Kippur, her kid brother looked up from his cereal and asked his parents: "Is Madeline Jewish?"

"WE WON. LET'S EAT."

Celebration

Two Texans are sitting on a plane going to Dallas with an old Jewish man sitting between them.

The first Texan says, "My name is Roger. I own 250,000 acres. I have 1,000 head of cattle and they call my place the Jolly Roger."

The second Texan says, "My name is John. I own 350,000 acres. I have 5,000 head of cattle and they call my place Big John's."

They both look down at the little old Jewish man, who says, "My name is Lenny Leibowitz and I own only 300 acres."

Roger looks down at him and says, "Three hundred acres? What do you raise?"

"Nothing," says Lenny.

"Well then, what do you call it?" asks John.

"Downtown Dallas."

A creature with green skin towers over all the other Bloomingdale's shoppers and is conspicuously covered with fancy jewelry. An older Jewish woman walks up to him and exclaims, in disbelief, how tall he is and how his skin is so green and how much jewelry is covering him, and asks, "Where are you from?" He responds, in perfect English, "I am from Mars." The woman sighs and says, "Ah. That explains your green skin." She goes on staring at him and her eyes veer up toward the ceiling, and she asks, "How tall are you?" Again, in perfect English and without missing a beat, he answers, "I am eight feet two inches tall." The woman asks if all Martians have green skin and are as tall as he is, and he says, "Yes. We all possess green skin and are all within a few inches of each other in height." "And do all of you wear so much jewelry?" she asks. The Martian responds: "Not the goyim."

F OR YEARS, Jewish jokes were looked at as repositories of self-hatred or masochism and despair. Freudian disciple Theodore Reik, in *Jewish Wit*, described them all as being about the "merciless mockery of weakness and faults and failing"; and psychoanalyst Martin Grotjahn, in a book-length essay titled *Psychoanalysis and the Jewish Joke*, called them "masochistic aggression turned against the self" and said they were "derived from the prevailing Gentile view of Jews." (Think Woody Allen seeing himself as a Hasid through Annie Hall's WASP grandmother's eyes.) Yet many of these jokes are celebrations of the ability to survive by whatever means are necessary. With mordant humor, they show a dogged resilience in the face of dreadful, even lethal adversity.

A Jew is told the earth will soon be flooded and all living

organisms will drown and die. He says he will begin to study how to live underwater.

Such a joke is really a celebration of Jewish survival.

Perhaps the longest surviving of all Jews, Mel Brooks's famous 2000 Year Old Man, claimed his longevity was the result of not eating fried food, not even touching it. He also took the idea of Jewish guilt to another level in his complaint to Carl Reiner that he had more than forty-two thousand children and not one had ever come to visit him.

Even the sometimes prescient Freud could never have foreseen the philo-Semitism that would temporarily emerge in the wake of the overwhelming sympathy for Jews engendered by the Second World War.

The source of Jewish humor has typically been located in a kind of masochism but also in suffering. It is self-deprecatory, and self-lacerating, and it sees Jews as outsiders, marginal people, victims.

Jewish jokes would become time capsules for the Jewish sense of being different and unique. And despite all the self-deprecation, there is a strain of celebration that often shows up, a healthy celebrating of escape from the oppression and prejudices of the past.

Jewish proverb: he that can't endure the bad will not live to see the good.

However . . . "Isn't Jewish humor masochistic?" an old joke begins, followed by the line "No. And if I hear that one more time, I'm going to kill myself."

Think of early comedians like Henny Youngman and the one-liners he made famous.

My doctor says to me: You're sick. I say: I want another opinion. He says: Okay. You're ugly, too.

Or Woody Allen telling us, early on in his career, that after he was born, the obstetrician slapped his mother. Or later on, saying that his parents rented out his room after he was kidnapped.

And then there was Rodney Dangerfield telling us his mother wouldn't breastfeed him. She only wanted to be friends.

He, too, had a tale about being kidnapped. The kidnappers sent his father a piece of his finger. His father, he said, wanted more proof.

The old axiom that Jewish parents walk closer to their children than non-Jews, suggesting their overprotectiveness, is turned on its head through the self-deprecatory joking of Youngman, Allen, and Dangerfield. They all seem to be saying: "I'm such a loser even my parents didn't want me." Joan Rivers claimed she knew she was an unwanted child because the bath toys her parents gave her were a toaster and a hair dryer.

But Jewish humor can also be celebratory. It celebrates what Jews have traditionally celebrated—food, family, wealth, success, and sobriety; sex and *naches* (joy); illustrious or heroic Jews; Jewish culture and Jewish mores; children; and, yes, even Jewish American princesses. All of these are, at times, stereotyped and ridiculed with sarcasm and aggression. Yet, notwithstanding even the darker and more acerbic side of Jewish jokes that poke merciless fun and make mincemeat of Jewish traits and Jewish neuroses, Jews celebrate that they are Jews and that they are alive.

Now, having a Martian use the word "goyim" is, in itself, a fairly funny punch line for a joke. But this joke, like a number of the so-called JAP (Jewish American princess) jokes, also celebrates difference and success. The joke is essentially telling us that a Jew, even if he is literally from another planet and 140 million miles from home, is still a Jew and not out of place at Bloomingdale's.

Jews will celebrate even when their numbers are depleted or they are unsure where their next meal is coming from. That is what I discovered on a trip to Cuba.

I was invited to Cuba by the San Francisco JCC, a trip set up before relations were officially renewed between Cuba and the United States. The trip was designed to help bring much-needed supplies to the small number of Jews remaining on the island, where the poverty was widespread and Jews, though they maintained and practiced Cuban and Jewish traditions in a lively and spirited way, were few in number.

Our group met with Adela Dworin, who was president of the Cuban Jewish community, and who showed us photos of Fidel Castro's visit to her offices in 2012 at the time that Pope Benedict VI was visiting the country and Castro had decided to mend fences with a number of Cuban religious leaders, including those of the Jews. I asked Señora Dworin in Spanish if she thought Castro might return and pay another visit. "*Sí sí*," she answered enthusiastically, and went on to explain to me that in 2012 she had invited him back for a Hanukkah celebration slated to take place the year we were there. "El Commandante did not know," she said, "what Hanukkah was," and then added that she had informed him, "It celebrates a revolution." Castro then, she reported, quickly snapped, "I will be there!"

We are in a kindergarten classroom. The teacher asks the class of five-year-olds to name the most famous man who ever lived and offers ten dollars to the child who provides the correct answer. A little Irish boy puts up his hand and says, "St. Patrick." The teacher says, "I'm sorry, Sean. That is not correct."

Then a little Scottish lad raises his hand and says, "St. Andrew," and the teacher says, "I'm sorry, Hamish, but that is also incorrect."

Whereupon a little Jewish boy raises his hand and says, "Jesus Christ," and the teacher says, "That is absolutely correct, Max. Congratulations! Please come up here and collect the ten dollars." As the teacher is giving Max the ten dollars, she says to him, "Since you are Jewish, Max, what made you say Jesus Christ?"

Max says to her, "In my heart I knew it was Moses, but business is business."

A classic joke, but also a joke with some radioactivity in it. On the face of it, the joke appears to be just another one about the Jews' talent for handling money. The implicit meaning of the joke lies in the fact that the Jewish kid understands how to play and adapt himself to a Christian audience (teacher and classmates), even in kindergarten, before children generally learn to read or write. But if we go deeper, the joke is also telling us that Jewish children, even at this rudimentary stage of education, have adopted an ethic that valorizes making money over expressing honest convictions and beliefs.

I had a strong personal reaction to this joke because, when I was a boy, my mother told me, "It's business," when I complained to her about my paternal aunt yelling at me for stacking baskets the wrong way in her husband's factory during my summer job. I was fond of my aunt and couldn't understand how someone who was always kind to me, whom my mother talked to daily on the telephone, and who sent me Hanukkah cards containing *gelt* (money) each year could yell at me. It was simple. To her there was no contradiction: her husband, my uncle, owned the factory. I was just another employee. My mother's response embodied the ethic that privileged business and moneymaking. Much of that ethic emerged from the Depression, but even before it, Americans heard their taciturn and dubbed as silent but admired president Calvin Coolidge say, "The business of America is business." And please, again, recall that Abraham Cahan's Jewish character David Levinsky was told, "In America you leave your *yichus* behind." That line, from *The Rise of David Levinsky,* the seminal Jewish American novel by the editor of the Yiddish daily the *Forward,* is a crystallization of the ethic I am describing here. *Yichus* refers to one's pedigree or family background and was, in the old country, tied to scholarly prestige or Torah learning. This, David Levinsky is told, means nothing in the United States, where cash is king. Bottom line from my mother? If it is in any way connected to business, even your own blood can yell at you.

But, again, consider the fact that Jews can celebrate and ridicule the stereotypes that for centuries had been turned against them. Perhaps the joke about Max and Jesus is even intimating, and yes, celebrating, something deep in Jewish character: "We learn this from the womb!" A scary thought? Yes. But there is also a kind of *naches* in thinking Jewish children show money smarts early on in their development.

Henny Youngman joked about money ethics being reflected in a simple, single question. If a businessperson, by a mistake, is given twice as much money as he's supposed to get, should he tell his partner?

A Jew who claims to have a talking and davening (praying in Hebrew) parrot (yet another davening parrot!) brags about the bird to all of his friends and fellow congregants, but no one believes him. They ridicule him until he takes bets that the parrot will daven at the next Friday-night service. He will show them the truth of his claims and collect his winnings. When the following Friday night rolls around, the man brings his parrot to shul, but despite much prodding, the parrot doesn't even make a single squawk. The man is enraged, berating the parrot as they leave the shul together, laughter and ridicule in their wake. "Now I'll have to pay off all those bets because you wouldn't daven," he says, in anger, when he and the parrot are by themselves. "Yes," says the parrot. "But think of how much we'll make taking bets on Yom Kippur."

Betting on Yom Kippur, the highest holy day of the year and a day linked to seeking God's forgiveness, would be extremely transgressive. (In an episode of Larry David's *Curb Your Enthusiasm,* a character scalps tickets to a Yom Kippur service.) But what stands out in the joke is a classic Jewish stereotype, the moneymaking shrewdness and cunning of the Jew in the form of a talking, davening parrot.

Nothing to do with money but I can't resist the temptation here to add another talking animal joke to the already significant number. It's the one about the Jewish man Larry Karp, who has a talking dog. He asks the dog to "Go fetch!" Instead of fetching, the dog berates the man with a barrage of complaints about how it doesn't get enough walks, Milk Bones, petting, or sniffing and running time with other dogs in the park. "What is this?" the owner asks his talking dog. "I simply asked you to go fetch." The talking Jewish dog says, "Oh, I'm sorry. I thought you said 'kvetch.'"

A Jew in a Texas bar wears a large Jewish star on a chain around his neck. A big, angry-looking Texan walks into the bar and spies the Jew and bellows, "I hate fucking Jews. Let's have a round for everyone in the bar except for the goddamned Jew." The Jew smiles. The Texan continues to order more rounds, one after another, for everyone, and he continues to exclude the Jew. Finally, with the Jew still smiling, and smiling broadly, the Texan says to the bartender, "What the hell is that damn Jew grinning about? I refuse to buy him a drink. Doesn't he realize how much I hate his Jew guts?" The bartender replies: "Yes, sir. But Mr. Bernstein is the owner."

In this and other Jewish jokes, including the other Texas one featuring Lenny, the owner of downtown Dallas, Jewish money wins out. Only in America, as the Jewish newspaper writer and publisher Harry Golden used to say, could Jew hating become major grist for the Jewish humor mill. Despite what for many might be the discomfort of such jokes, the freedom that has given birth to them surely is worth celebrating. As is Bernstein's ownership of the bar . . . which makes a sap of the big Texan Jew hater.

A wealthy Jew lives next door to the famed banker and extraordinarily wealthy philanthropist J. P. Morgan. Both have enormous estates and the Jewish neighbor has the same cars as Morgan, the same landscaping, and a replica of Morgan's gigantic pool. This copycat behavior annoys Morgan, and one day he bluntly and angrily says to his Jewish neighbor, "Are you trying to be my equal? Do you actually believe you can be my equal by copying me?" The Jew responds, "I am not your equal. I am better than you!" Morgan acidly asks, "And why is that?" "Because," says Morgan's Jewish neighbor, "I don't have a Jew living next to me."

This joke always fascinated me. J. P. Morgan, the banker and financier of Croesus-like wealth in the late nineteenth and early twentieth centuries, actually had a real rivalry with Jewish bankers of his time. Morgan made many anti-Semitic comments in his correspondence to the effect that Jews were not white, this at a time when nonwhite immigrants could not become citizens. (It's all in Susie Pak's book *Gentleman Banker: The World of J. P. Morgan.*) The joke is striking in that, once again, we have a Jew of great wealth managing to get in the last word against a rival whom he is, nonetheless, emulating. The joke celebrates a quick-witted, highly successful Jew who succeeds in putting down a legendary tycoon, a so-called captain of industry, by using his own Jewishness and Morgan's anti-Semitism. Though the Jew in the joke is a copycat, he is one with chutzpah as well as capital.

A young Jewish boy goes off to college and is told by his father to date only Jewish girls lest he fall in love with and marry a shiksa, a girl who is not Jewish. The boy meets a Gentile girl and falls in love. To his father's chagrin, he marries the girl, who converts to Judaism and becomes a devout, practicing Jew. They have children. The father calls his son one day, informs him he has purchased a new boat, and invites the son and the son's family for what promises to be a wonderful day of sailing. The son reminds his father that it is Shabbos and his wife, being highly observant, will not be able to join them. The father says, "I told you to marry a Jewish girl!"

The obvious humor is in the fact that the son's wife, a convert, is now more of a Jew than the Jewish father or his son. Implicit in the joke, too, is the hope, a wish really, that Jewish practice will endure despite legitimate Jewish fears about loss through intermarriage. The joke also tells us implicitly that if Jewish practice and observance are lost, it may be because Jews by birth, not converts, abandon religious laws and rituals. Built into the joke is the image of success and prosperity evoked by the father's boat.

Jackie Mason, in one of his early routines, had shtick about Jews buying boats only to show off to their friends how many passengers the boat could accommodate, not for actual use—because boating, like skiing and a number of other sports, is often joked about as not being for Jews. Lenny Bruce, however, said in one of his many lists of what is Jewish versus what is goyish, that skiing is Jewish while snowmobiling is goyish. All of this, once again, is a form of insistence on Jewish difference. Lenny Bruce on food: Chocolate is Jewish and fudge is goyish.

Fruit salad is Jewish. Lime Jell-O is goyish. Pumpernickel is Jewish. White bread is very goyish. Instant potatoes, goyish. Black cherry soda and macaroons, very Jewish.

The joke reminds me of the time *New York Times* columnist and PBS talking head David Brooks explained to me how he had tried to move away from his Jewish background by becoming increasingly secular and marrying an Episcopalian, only to have his wife not only convert to Judaism but ultimately become a rabbi. He thought, when he told me this, of the line in *Godfather III*, when Al Pacino's Michael Corleone says: "Just when I thought I was out, they keep pulling me back in."

A private Boeing 747 full of Jews lands in Katmandu. The passengers are all friends or relations of the Weinberger family and the special limousines that pick them up are headed some one hundred kilometers away to the foot of the Himalayas. They are all in India for the bar mitzvah of little Stevie Weinberger, what many are calling the über bar mitzvah, or the bar mitzvah to outdo all other bar mitzvahs, a bar mitzvah so exotic, costly, and lavish that it will upend and outspend any previous bar mitzvah—which is really saying something! The rental of the 747 and the fleet of limos—who can even estimate the cost of it all? When the guests exit the limos, there are long lines of elephants, each led by a young Indian elephant trainer, to take them, even the few who are elderly and infirm, one by one, to the base of the mountains. The elephants and their attendants are accompanied by teams of bejeweled dancing women, a group of Sufi whirling dervishes, and a long line of Sherpas flown in from Tibet. A separate jet has brought in an incalculable amount of specially catered food—including Stevie's favorite, lean-cut corned beef sandwiches, in state-of-the-art wheeled-in refrigerators. The women dance, a bevy of musicians from yet another rented jet and limo play Stevie's favorite songs, and the elephants march forward to the Himalayas.

The team of elephants is about to begin their ascent. All the guests, each on top of an elephant, are being led toward an area on the side of the mountains where a miniature Taj Mahal is visible. The Weinberger family are at the front of the procession.

Suddenly a group of Indian men in uniforms are wildly waving batons and holding up the procession

as the elephants are about to move toward the minia-
ture Taj Mahal.

Stevie's father, Mr. Weinberger, is distressed. He
asks the Indian officers what is going on and why ev-
eryone has been commanded to stop. "We have a bar
mitzvah celebration," Stevie's dad says forcefully to
them. "Everyone has been paid. What's the holdup?"

The Indian officer closest to him, who is clearly in
charge, shrugs his shoulders and says: "I'm terribly
sorry, sir. We'll all just have to wait a little while until
the Goldstein bar mitzvah party ends."

Another joke about ostentatious spending by rich Jews, and
in the joke, too, is a reference to the competition among Jews
to outdo each other. Some bar mitzvahs clearly have been way
over-the-top, doubtless a source of pride for some Jews, espe-
cially those throwing the party.

Love of money has become the root of much present-day
Jewish humor. Jokes about Jews having or spending a lot or
Jews being tightwads have nearly become a staple for a lot
of young Jewish comics looking for a laugh at the expense
(so to speak) of the stereotypes. Anti-Semitic stereotypes
show Jews as huge and lavish spenders but also as tightfisted
misers. Jews are cast both as Communists and capitalists.

I've always wondered how both stereotypes, mutually exclusive, continue to thrive.

A Jewish son tells his father he has seen the bicycle of his dreams in a local bike shop on sale for $200. Can his father please please please buy it for him? His father first says, "Whoever heard of a bike costing $170? I would need to borrow to buy a $150 bike. What can you possibly hope to get in a bike for $120?" I've heard that joke, in varying versions, from younger Jews, who tell it with enthusiasm for the idea it embodies of Jews being cheap and, as the joke suggests, teaching cheapness diligently to their children. Here's another one like it, but less funny: What is the absolute favorite thing for Jewish football fans to see? Answer: they like most seeing the defensive players on their team get the quarterback. Or the one about Jews liking to watch porn movies backward because they like the part where the hooker gives the money back.

Silly, right? Yes. But also revealing of a tectonic shift. It is as if pride in those traits that once caused discomfort to Jews have somehow become worth celebrating. My sister-in-law told the story of being in an apartment in Manhattan. She is saying good-bye to her father-in-law, a hardworking businessman, a rough-around-the-edges type who no one, least of all my sister-in-law, would ever associate with any glimmering of knowledge of the world of the arts or culture. When he asks her where she is going, she tells him she is going to MoMA, the Museum of Modern Art.

> Him: Why are you going there?
> Her: There is a special exhibit I want to see.
> Him: Exhibit of what?
> Her: Of Monet.
> Him: Oh. I know all about Monet.
> Her (in mild disbelief): You do? You know all about Monet?
> Him (extracting a fat wad of bills from his pants pocket and flipping through them). Yeah. Monet! Monet!

I would never subscribe to the notion that there is any basis to what some might call Jews' love of money. As a young man, I was appalled to hear a couple of Gentile acquaintances talk about "Jewing someone down," or of someone "being Jewed down." I called one guy I was friendly with out on his use of those phrases and he told me he never even realized and it never dawned on him they were in any way connected to the Jewish people or the religion. Of course this was in southern Ohio in the sixties, where a fellow in my dorm named Zeke honestly believed Jews had horns. But a joke like the one about the father continuing to reduce the cost of the bike, and even the joke about getting the "quarter back" or the one about wanting to see a hooker give money back—all are anchored in a stereotype of Jewish cheapness and love of money that stubbornly persists and that some Jews now like to joke about while others still condemn.

I also recall from my college days buying a round or two of beers for Gentiles, taking the role of an unpaid PR agent, working on behalf of my brethren, just to show that Jews weren't cheap, and doing so nearly religiously (so to speak) even though I had little if any money and did not particularly like beer.

However much Jews spend or don't spend, earn or don't earn, they will doubtless always be connected to stereotypes of being rich and/or cheap with money. Or, worse, shifty and deceitful with it, the all-Jews-are-Bernie-Madoff equation. The fear, of course, is that even joking about such stereotypes can reinforce them or cause pain. But what should be said of the freedom that comes with expressing, perhaps even owning and celebrating them, with humor?

Money was associated by most immigrants with the American dream. The Chinese emigrated with the myth of America being a gold mountain, and many Jews who came from

Europe and other parts of the world believed American streets were lined with gold. I recall an Afghan immigrant store owner telling some young kids who couldn't pay for the items they'd brought to the counter: "No money, no honey, in America." When my high school friend Susan Venig's grandfather escaped to America from Germany and was asked his name, he thought he was being asked how much money he had since everything he had heard about America was tied to money. His last name was Howard. Not knowing a word of English, he told the immigration officer he had twelve pfennig. Which is how the family name became Venig.

America enabled many Jews to become rich or simply prosperous; it was, of course, for many a dream come true. A Yiddish word, *alevai*, which means "I hope" or "I wish" or "if only" appears in many contexts. Leo Rosten uses the example of the Jew who says if God would only give him $10,000 (maybe $20,000 by today's standards), he would promise to give a thousand of it to the poor, *alevei*! But if God didn't trust him, God could deduct a thousand in advance and simply give him the balance.

A black woman tries on mink coat after mink coat, each coat being more expensive than the one before

it. Finally, she is told by the saleslady waiting on her that she will be shown the most expensive and sought-after mink in the store. A full-length coat, complete with a variety of jewels, is brought to her by one of the store's floor people and she tries it on and examines herself in a large mirror. She poses, repeatedly, walking back and forth in front of the mirror, studying her reflection. The saleslady comes up, compliments her, and reminds her that this particular coat is the most expensive one they have and, she adds, likely one of the most costly minks in all of the United States, possibly in the world. The black woman looks again at her image in the mirror, pauses, then asks: "I don't know. Do you think it makes me look too Jewish?"

Even in jokes involving other ethnic groups Jews are the gold-standard stereotype of wealth.

Yes, many Jews in America and other developed nations have succeeded and are prosperous beyond the wildest dreams of their forefathers and foremothers. Many are also no longer mortally afraid of upsetting Gentiles ("What will the goyim think?") or stirring up anti-Semitism, bringing undue attention to the wealth of any in their tribe.

As for the spending habits of Jews. . . . A Jew suddenly finds himself by the entrance to a time machine, thrown back to Roman antiquity and placed inside a Roman galley, rowing with other slaves under a Roman soldier's whip. The Jew turns to the slave next to him and asks, "How much are we supposed to tip the whipper?"

A rabbi, on the occasion of his synagogue's fortieth anniversary, announces to his congregation that, despite his leadership role and all of the success he and the synagogue have had, he feels he is a nothing. Whereupon a high-profile attorney stands up and says that he, too, one of the synagogue's original founders, has achieved far more success than he ever would have imagined but feels he, too, is a nothing. Then a doctor, another of the original founders and a much-respected and successful physician, stands up and says, "I, too, despite all my achievements and successes, feel I am a nothing." Finally, the synagogue's shammash, its lowly janitor, rises from among the seated congregants and says he has been with the synagogue since its founding and also feels he is a nothing. The rabbi points at him with disdain and says, "Look who thinks he's a nothing!"

Well you might ask, Why is that joke funny? Even with success and abundant wealth, all for sure worth celebrating, there is still competition with Jews of lower stature as well as the ever-present anxiety about really being nothing. But the joke reveals that even in feeling as though one is a nothing, one can still in reality be a somebody, with accomplishments well worth celebrating.

A Jew is sitting on a park bench eating matzo. He sees a blind man on a bench across from him. Out of kindness and concern, he goes over to the blind man and, assuming the man is hungry, hands him a piece of his matzo. The blind man slowly touches the matzo, feeling it all along its surface, even its ridges, and then exclaims, "You read this shit?"

The joke reminds me of a true story. I was once having lunch in a deli in Marin County with my friend Dr. Dean Edell, long a popular radio and television medical adviser.

Dean ordered matzo brie and the waitress brought him Brie cheese on matzo.

At the time, I thought that would have been a great anecdote for Herb Caen, the veteran three-star San Francisco columnist. He loved stories like it, with its humor referencing a place like Marin County, where you could well imagine such a misunderstanding taking place.

But back to the joke!

On the surface, it celebrates *tzedakah* and makes us aware of what matzo feels like and its obvious connection to Passover. But matzo has been given other, far more baleful interpretations throughout history. The joke has a deeper undercurrent, beyond the allusions to braille and *tzedakah*, for Jews were persecuted for centuries in the false belief that matzo was made from the blood of Christian infants. The blunt "You read this shit?" evokes a fecal association with matzo that challenges the real purpose of the man's generosity in giving the blind man food—an action that, on its own, Jews celebrate as a true mitzvah.

On the other hand, to borrow from Freud, who said sometimes a cigar is just a cigar: sometimes a piece of matzo is just a piece of matzo. Sometimes a joke is just a joke.

Jackie Mason had many jokes about Jews eating and celebrating special occasions with enormous amounts of food while

Gentiles were, he claimed, principally interested in consuming liquor. That kind of material goes back to the idea that Jews, unlike Gentiles, are supposedly not shickers (drunkards). The idea connects all the way back to the shtetl and pogroms, often led by drunken Cossacks or other drunken non-Jews. "Oy yoi yoi, the shicker is the goy," the old adage right out of the shtetl, literally means the non-Jew is the drunk.

I remember telling my mother that Eugene O'Neill's great Irish American tragedy, *Long Day's Journey into Night,* with all of its ambivalence, guilt, and blame, had parallels to our Jewish family. After she saw the play, my mother said, "Honey, we aren't like those people. We don't drink."

But Jews do love food and celebrate it with a good deal of humor. I managed to get the actor Alan Arkin to laugh uncontrollably when, during an interview with him, I asked him if he remembered an interview he did many years before on CBS when he was asked what his favorite role was. He couldn't recall what he said. So I reminded him that his answer was "a kaiser roll."

A longtime Jewish woman friend of mine named Judith Rich tells the story of her mother's sister on

board a train with a lunch her mother had packed for her to eat. An old Jewish man was seated near her and the aunt offered to share her lunch with him. The old man said no until he saw some *kichel* (a Jewish cookie) and then said yes. When he tasted it, he said to her, "You must be Rivka Nevelson's granddaughter." She was.

Okay. So maybe it's more a story than a joke. But the line is thin between the two and sometimes nonexistent. Sharing your lunch with an older stranger is a good example of *tzedakah*, which, once again, is a mitzvah worthy of celebration. What beside generosity would motivate someone to do that? The story not only shows the closeness of a community, but the special pride in women being good *balabostas* (homemakers), especially where Jewish baking is concerned. Thus we have, in Judith's family tale, an ascending order of values from the generosity of *tzedakah* to the importance of community to the strength of the memory of Jewish baked food—in this case, appropriately enough, a baked sweet.

So let us go to another true tale from the wide world of Jewish humor. I mention it because it is indicative of what many Jews have celebrated as long as they have celebrated food and wine and the Jewish holidays

I like to tell the story. It is about a boyhood chum from my Cleveland neighborhood whom we called Pissy. I went to visit him when we were both in college in Ohio. I drove up from Athens to the state capital in Columbus, where both Ohio State and Pissy were located. When I found his apartment, I parked my car in front and saw him run out. I assumed he was excited to see me, but as it turned out, he wanted to brief me, hastily and with obvious anxiety, about the fact that he had a live-in Christian girlfriend who didn't know he was a Jew. He begged me, with great seriousness, not to mention, under any circumstances, his being Jewish. I gave him my solemn word that I would not say the words "Jew" or "Jewish."

When I met the young lady, who was amiable and, I should add, wearing a large cross, I asked her if she knew how talented Fred (Pissy's real name) was at making kreplach for matzo ball soup. She looked puzzled. I went on. "Not only does he make a great kreplach, he is a master of charoset and all Pesach dishes and can bake a wonderful challah for an Oneg Shabbat."

Pissy was pissed! But I had kept my word and had not uttered the words "Jew" or "Jewish." I felt he deserved my shtick with the Jewish food words for concealing his Jewishness. I don't believe the young woman had much of an idea of what any of the Jewish food words meant or what culture they belonged to.

These stories stay in my quiver like jokes, humorous when told and retold but also rooted in a sense of nostalgia and in my own Jewish identity. Most Jews have a staple of such stories that they tell and retell in ways that celebrate memory.

Froggy, also my neighbor, and I were what my bubbie would have called a pair of *paskunyaks,* a great Yiddish word denoting evil or horrible, but used more often affectionately about bad-boy mischief makers. Froggy was getting bar mitzvah lessons from an itinerant rabbi whose name was Katz, whom we called Rabbi Katz-in-*tuchas,* meaning Rabbi Katz in the ass. A little man with a huge skull, the rabbi would park his old Studebaker blocks away on Shabbos. He would sneak over to Froggy's house or to the homes of others in the neighborhood who he was tutoring at his hourly rate, making everyone believe he walked on Shabbos because driving was forbidden. Froggy and I one Saturday found his car parked and unlocked. We climbed in and planted ourselves across the seats, he in the front, and I in the back. We knew Katz-in-*tuchas* was taking his usual surreptitious route back, and when he opened the front door on the driver's side, we popped up and greeted him in unison with "*Gut yuntif,* Rabbi." Katz-in-*tuchas* clutched his heart. I honestly thought for a few moments we had killed him.

Just the name Katz can make me laugh. I went to Hebrew school with a funny troublemaker named Teddy Katz. The teacher, a volatile and short-tempered man, once ordered class-disrupting Teddy to stand in the corner. As Teddy stood there, he suddenly, audibly, began to sing the lyrics to "Jesus Loves Me," which actually caused our wildly incensed Hebrew teacher to froth at the mouth.

I certify both Katz stories are true. The memory of either or both, to the present day, can make me laugh. As much as a good Jewish joke.

A bus filled with dedicated Hadassah ladies is traveling through the Southwest and goes off a cliff, instantly killing everyone on the bus. All of the women ascend to heaven, where they find a young intern is filling in for St. Peter. St. Peter appears, hours later, back at his post at the entrance to heaven and God shows up a couple of days later asking where the Hadassah ladies are. It turns out that the young intern made a dreadful mistake and sent all of them, every one of them, to hell. When God hears this, he gets on the emergency phone to Satan and tells the devil right off that a bevy of Hadassah ladies were sent by mistake straight to hell. "I know," says Lucifer. "Already they've raised enough money to air-condition this place."

Actually, I wanted to end this chapter with this particular joke because many wonderful Jewish women have devoted their adult lives to organizations such as Hadassah, my mother being one of them. Because of economics and two-worker marriages, the number of these women, who are well worth celebrating, has declined. Over the years I have noted how their ranks, once so large in number, have thinned. But the joke speaks volumes about the admirable dedication and zeal of Hadassah ladies and their ability to get things done.

When the Oscar-winning film director Barry Levinson lived in Marin County, where I lived for many years, we periodically saw each other for lunch. He got me one day to tell Jewish jokes nonstop to Dustin Hoffman, who loved hearing them, when they were filming Michael Crichton's *Sphere* in Vallejo, a film my dad would unhesitatingly have branded with the Yiddish "from *cockin*," meaning from shit. As my dad would say, and I would agree, Levinson made far better films: *Diner; Avalon; Rain Man; Good Morning, Vietnam; Bugsy;* and many others.

Levinson and I enjoyed each other's company and talked a good deal about politics and current events. He told me a lot of Hollywood stories. When he told me one day he was going back to his hometown of Baltimore and, thanks to his mother, would be addressing hundreds of Hadassah ladies there, he wanted to know if I knew any Jewish jokes that would be appropriate for the occasion.

I told Levinson the perfect joke. The one about the Hadassah ladies in the bus. He told me afterward the joke went over well.

But I want to tell you about my own experience with a far smaller number of Hadassah ladies in Marin County. The chapter's president had been after me for months to give a pro bono talk. As I said, I have always admired the work Hadassah women do. My own experience talking to the Marin Hadassah is a story for the ages.

The chapter president, who had pleaded with me to be their featured speaker, showed up with a couple of other women to greet me. One of them, let's call her Mrs. Zaftig, grabbed hold of me by my arm and said, "It's my favorite talk-show host, Michael Krasnell." I realized she was pulling me away from

the others, actually woman-handling me, so to speak, urging
me to meet her husband, Al, who suddenly appeared looking
as if he had been airlifted straight from Miami Beach—he
was wearing an open shirt with white chest hair and a huge
gold *chai* poking through, white shoes, and white hair with a
panama hat. "You gotta meet Al. You gotta meet Al," she kept
squawking as Al just stood there, immobile, staring at me with
a dumb frozen smile. "Al is a big fan, too," she assured me.

Next thing I know I'm giving my talk. I'm not going to
play false modest. I give good talks—animated, energetic, and
engaging—but this one was distracting. There was a young
couple seated in the front row of the auditorium, and the
young woman was babbling to the young man seated next to
her from the moment I began speaking. This couple stood out
because everyone else in the crowd was older. I kept talking,
but finally I could not restrain myself and nicely and politely
asked the young woman if she would be considerate enough
to stop talking. "If you need to talk to the gentleman next to
you," I added, I thought graciously, "perhaps you might want
to talk outside." I thanked her and she stopped talking. But
only for a minute or two. Her yakking to the young man next
to her continued right up to the end of my talk, at which point
the woman who had pleaded with me to give the talk came
running over. I assumed she was going to thank me for what I

felt certain was a good talk. Instead, she said, "How could you talk to my daughter-in-law so insultingly? You have no idea how hard I had to work to get her to come today. And she's not even Jewish. But I taught her how to make gefilte fish and she makes it great!"

Is that a Jewish story? Or does it sound eerily similar to a Jewish joke?

All Jewish holidays can be described in nine words. Those nine words? THEY TRIED TO KILL US. WE WON. LET'S EAT.

I call the nine-word summation of the Jewish past a great joke because it brings to the fore associations with Jewish holidays and eating, whether after fasting on Yom Kippur or sitting through a Haggadah service before a seder meal. It also serves to link Jews to their history, all set against the impatience of the non-Orthodox Jews of the contemporary period, who, like my father, rushed through seders to get to the meal. (If you listened to the comic Jackie Mason you would assume all Jews want to do is eat while all Gentiles want to do is drink.)

Notwithstanding one year, in the early seventies, when

friends introduced feminist Hagaddahs to their seder—which brought a lot of bad jokes about bra burning—traditional seders, just like eating and being fed, are identified with Jewish women, who, until the most recent wave of feminism changed traditional roles, did all of the work and preparing. The novelist Cynthia Ozick once quipped that the exodus may have freed Jews from pharaoh's slavery, but it did not free Jewish women from the slave work required of them to prepare the home for Passover and cook for the seder.

Embedded in the nine-word joke, too, is the joy associated with the communal Passover experience reflected in those last two words: "Let's eat." What is lost in tradition is made up for in the present with speed and abundance. The real essence of the joke is in the juxtaposition of the Jewish past with the immediacy of wanting to eat. Most major Jewish holidays, with the exceptions of Hanukkah and Purim, are, in fact, not about others trying to kill all of the Jews. In fact, in the ancient past, which is hallowed at Passover seders, it is God who does the killing—of the Egyptian firstborn. Thanks to God parting the Red Sea and Moses leading the children of Israel, the Bible teaches, Jews managed to escape to freedom. I remember one Passover seder when I first heard the quip that points out the real difference between Christianity and Judaism: JESUS

SAVES. MOSES INVESTS. And, speaking of Moses, remember, too, that Woody Allen in *Love and Death* says if only he could witness a miracle, like the parting of the Red Sea by God or Moses talking to the Burning Bush or his uncle Sasha picking up a check.

Of course we have come to a point where the entire story of the Jews being enslaved in Egypt has been questioned by lack of archaeological evidence and the story of Passover posited as merely a myth. Fast-forward from pharaoh's time to 1967, and the making of *Funny Girl* and the Six-Day War between Israel and Egypt. The film, under William Wyler's direction, faced serious obstacles brought on by the fact that Barbra Streisand's leading man was the Egyptian actor Omar Sharif. Streisand's Jewish mother was quoted as saying, "My daughter isn't going to work with an Egyptian." When a leading Egyptian newspaper, discussing Omar Sharif's being cast as Streisand's leading man, screamed out the headline EGYPT ANGRY!, Streisand said, "Egypt angry? You should hear what my aunt Sarah says." The movie got made and Egyptians, furious at their native son Sharif, spoke for a while of taking away his citizenship for kissing a Jewish woman. Though both were married, Streisand and Sharif allegedly fell in love on the set. In 1992, Streisand would do a memorable walk-on as herself during a *Saturday Night Live* skit where three cartoonish middle-aged

Jewish mothers played by Mike Meyers, Madonna, and Rose-anne Barr all claim to be *farklempt* over her not winning an Oscar for *The Prince of Tides*.

Naches over Streisand's Jewishness is, of course, another clear example of Jews celebrating the success of one of their own. Will Jews ever celebrate having one of their own as the first Jewish American president of the United States? A singular fact separating Jews in America from Gentiles remains the fact that only Gentiles have been presidents. In spite of all the Jewish mothers, including mine, who told their sons any boy could grow up to be president, no Jewish boy ever has.

When Connecticut senator Joseph Lieberman was nominated to run with then vice president Al Gore, the thought occurred to many Jews that there might one day be a Jewish president. Eliot Spitzer, once a New York governor and a tough Wall Street prosecutor, was considered a possibility to become the first Jewish president until, as I told him bluntly in an interview I did with him after a scandal with a hooker killed his political career, "You blew it, Governor."

Soon after Vermont senator Bernie Sanders announced his run for the presidency, I asked him which he thought would turn away more voters—his being a socialist or a Jew. Bernie answered immediately, "A socialist," though he added that he was a Democratic socialist like those in Scandinavia. Which is why some wag suggested Bernie should run instead for president of Denmark or Sweden. A photo of Sanders went viral after he announced his run for the 2016 presidency with the caption, "They tell me Bernie Sanders can't win because America won't vote for a Socialist Jew/I tell them America celebrates a Socialist Jew every December 25."

Responding to criticism of being anti-Israel and even anti-Semitic, President Barack Obama, the nation's first African American chief executive, according to what his confidant and adviser David Axelrod told me, said," I am the closest thing to a Jew that has ever sat in this office." In *You Could Live If They Let You,* by the Jewish American novelist Wallace Markfield, the stand-up comic protagonist says: "The time is at hand when the wearing of a prayer shawl and a skullcap will not bar a man from the White House—unless, of course, that man is Jewish."

That day when a Jew sits in the Oval Office may one day come. But in the meantime, as many Jewish jokes reveal, there is much to celebrate. Perhaps most of all is celebration of *chai,* the Hebrew word for life, oddly enough often associated with Elvis Presley, who habitually wore a gold *chai* on a chain around his neck. The word is tied most of all to the life force and the tree of life, which is to say to God the creator. Sheldon

Harnick's lyric in *Fiddler on the Roof* is key. Tevye sings, in his toast at his daughter's wedding, "Here's to our prosperity. Our good health and happiness. And most important, to life. *L'chaim!*" In life there can be laughter and in laughter there is life worth celebrating.

Suffering

An old Jew is kvetching about being thirsty. "Oy, am I thirsty," he moans. He says it over and over again. "Oy, am I thirsty." Finally, someone hands him a glass of water. He gulps it down. Then he says, "Oy, vas I thirsty."

Following an especially arduous hike, the Russian says, "I'm tired and I'm thirsty. I must have vodka," while the German says, "I'm tired and I'm thirsty. I must have beer," and the Frenchman says, "I'm tired and I'm thirsty. I must have wine." The Mexican says, "I'm tired and I'm thirsty. I must have tequila." The Jew says, "I'm tired and I'm thirsty. I must have diabetes."

MOST OF the Jewish jokes that have endured in the United States, Western Europe, and Israel derive from the Ashkenazi experience and are concerned with the gulf between past and present. As the Christian theologian Paul Tillich once remarked, Jews are a people of time. Or, to frame it in a joke that Isaac Bashevis Singer, the Nobel Prize–winning Yiddish novelist, once told me: "Jews suffer from every disease except amnesia."

Yiddish, perhaps more than any other language, is rife not only with curses but with words of lamentation: words like *tsuris* (trouble, misery, or aggravation) and verbs such as kvetch (to complain) and *geschrei* (to wail). All of these words go snugly with "oy," a word that includes a vast range of aches, pains, and suffering.

Philip Roth's Portnoy memorably said he wanted to put the oy in goy and the id in Yid. In other words, for Gentiles to be the ones to have to suffer and feel guilt, as Jews do, and for Jews to be guilt-free and unbridled in pleasure seeking. Portnoy also wanted, he told his shrink, Dr. Spielvogel, his people to take their suffering and shove it.

Even suffering is turned by Jews into jokes. A doctor tells his patient he has bad news: the patient has cancer and a serious heart condition. But there is also good news, the doctor enthuses: "You aren't a hypochondriac." According to a Jewish headstone, "I told you I was sick." Jewish humor, with its irony and wit, can extend to the finality of death and even beyond, as in the allegedly true tale I read in a book on sports trivia by Larry Stone, about the fan who took his grievances and disappointment with the perennially losing Cubs to the grave. Buried near Wrigley Field in Chicago, the man requested three words in Yiddish on his gravestone, words that translate to "the Cubs stink."

The Jewish comedian Billy Crystal turns death's sting into humor in *700 Sundays*, the poignant autobiography and one-man Tony Award–winning show about the death of his father when Billy was fifteen. He does this by mimicking the lisping voice of the funeral director who says, "My condolenchess to the family of the decheassed." It prompts Crystal to complain, "My father is dead and I have to talk to Sylvester the Cat?" Suffering turned into a one-liner.

Anti-Semitism, a source of great pain and suffering for centuries, can also be turned into a source of humor, as in the joke I relished as a young broadcaster about the Jewish guy who tries out for a job as an announcer and is not hired. When asked by an acquaintance why he thought he didn't get the job, the would-be announcer says, "Anti-Ssssssemitism."

My sister, Lois, was having dinner in a Cleveland restaurant called the Wagon Wheel. People seated next to her were saying things that were downright anti-Semitic. She couldn't believe what she was hearing. "They are so damn cheap" and "I can't believe how clannish they are." It was painful and distressing to her as the comments continued. Finally, when the dinner was over and the Jew haters were ready to leave, she swallowed hard, boldly went up to them, and said: "I couldn't help overhearing what you were saying during dinner and it was disgusting. I want you to know that I heard it all and I am Jewish." Whereupon one of the women, who had been seated at the table, piped up and said, "So are we!" And another added, "Yes. We all are."

Past stereotypes have been viciously used against Jews, even by their fellow tribe members. The chief source of Jew hatred may now be tied to Israel, but for centuries it was due largely to their rejection of Jesus as lord and savior. They were tortured and murdered for supposedly killing Christ—which, despite Mel Gibson's film, they did not have much (if any) of a hand in. Yet even that libel can be turned into a kind of humor. My dad swore that when some hoods in his high school were after him, calling him a Christ killer, he said, "It wasn't me. I was at the ball game." The charge of being Christ killers has, of course, plagued Jews through the millennia even though Jesus was a Jew, which has been an ongoing source of humor—as in the joke about the group of Hasids who show up to the Catholic ceremony of a nun being wed to Christ. They sit in the front row claiming they are relatives on the groom's side.

Even the Crucifixion can be turned into humor. Like the joke about the Crucifixion of Christ taking place in modern times—by electrocution, not by order of Pontius Pilate. Would Christians then, the joke asks, wear a small electric chair on a chain around their necks rather than a cross?

The famed comedian Lenny Bruce joked that the Jews should be let off the hook for killing Christ because of the statute of limitations. He also claimed, "We killed him because a party got out of hand" and "he didn't want to become a doctor." Bruce also claimed his family found a note in their basement confessing to their killing Christ and signed by Morty.

If humor can be created out of the actual Crucifixion, then the possibilities, especially for humor of a darker nature, begin to expand nearly exponentially to many other once forbidden topics. A group of Jewish writers, including such early figures as Nathanael West (née Nathan Weinstein) of *Miss Lonelyhearts* and *Day of the Locust* fame, and later on, Jewish novelists like Joseph Heller (the author of *Catch-22*) or Bruce Jay Friedman (the author of *Stern* and *A Mother's Kisses*) became associated with what was called black humor—which had nothing to do with Richard Pryor, Dick Gregory, or, heaven forbid, Bill Cosby. It was (and remains) a kind of dark or gallows humor that, paradoxically, can act as a kind of balm for pain and suffering and was especially significant in works by a number of non-Jewish American writers like Flannery O'Connor, Kurt Vonnegut, and Thomas Pynchon. The darker the humor the more comic writers began not only to welcome and love it, but even to celebrate it.

Humor even has emerged out of the Holocaust. How can this event, the Shoah, be a source of humor? As the well-circulated line among Jews in the entertainment industry goes: "There's no business like Shoah business."

Let's remember Ricky Gervais presenting Kate Winslet a

214 Let There Be Laughter

Golden Globe and saying to her, "Well done, Winslet. I told you, do a Holocaust movie and awards come, didn't I?" Gervais, who is not Jewish, was pushing the envelope hard on the Jews-run-Hollywood cliché, which many see as an anti-Semitic canard. A year later, after hosting the Golden Globes, Gervais concluded with "shalom from me and Mel Gibson."

Early in his career, after the notorious Nazi criminal Adolf Eichmann had been captured, put on trial in Jerusalem, and executed, Woody Allen said they found his (Woody's) name and phone number in Eichmann's pants pocket. Jack Benny, in a similar vein, said he agreed with Will Rogers that he never met a man he didn't like, then added, "Well, maybe Eichmann."

The movie director Judd Apatow, who gave us such films as *The 40-Year-Old Virgin* and *Knocked Up*, for years wanted to do stand-up. He showed up on *The Tonight Show* with a routine after the release of the Amy Schumer film *Trainwreck*, which he directed. With Jewish self-deprecation, he compared a perfect drawing of himself to Nazi propaganda.

I heard Harvard Yiddish professor Ruth Wisse tell a Holocaust joke, apparently quite popular in Israel during a rash of suicide bombings. Morbid or gallows humor? Yes. But think of the irony! The joke is about a suicide bomb going off in a Jerusalem café near the home of relatives of an American Jewish family. The concerned American relatives call and are assured that everyone in the house is safe. They ask about the teenage daughter, Hodel, who they knew hung out at that particular café. They are told, "Hodel is fine. She's safe. She's at Auschwitz."

Built out of the ashes of concentration camps like Auschwitz, Israel had become a deadly place for Jewish children, while Auschwitz, which many young Jewish students continue to visit, had turned into a safe place!

The fact is, Holocaust humor, like humor about Anti-Semitism, is mostly no longer forbidden, especially if the jokes come from Jews themselves rather than someone like Ricky Gervais or, much worse, Mel Gibson. It can be a touchy question as to who tells such jokes and gets a pass and who does not. The real subtext of the humor, however, is simple and direct. Out of suffering, humor can emerge.

Years ago I introduced Elie Wiesel, the Nobel Peace Prize–winning Holocaust survivor and author. After Wiesel had given a talk, a man came up to him. The man turned out to have been with him in Auschwitz. It was an incredible unforeseen reunion. After hugging and crying, they began to talk about the SS Nazi guard who beat them. Each summoned memories of how violent and sadistic the guard had been. Then, as they compared remembrances, they suddenly began to talk about his peculiar and bizarre personal habits and then, uncontrollably, they began to laugh. It was an extraordinary sight to witness and showed me how humor can emerge many years later even from terrible suffering.

In America and other developed countries, Jews were at last free of persecution, pogroms, and genocide. All of that suffering became grist for the humor mill, even in a controversial joke like the one Joan Rivers told on *Fashion Police* about German supermodel Heidi Klum's neckline-plunging gold dress. Rivers was condemned for the remark by the Anti-Defamation League and refused to apologize for saying, while on the red carpet, "The last time a German looked this hot was when they were pushing Jews into the ovens." Rivers defended the joke, saying that many of the members of her husband Edgar's family were killed in the Holocaust and she would never apologize for reminding people of it.

In an episode of Larry David's *Curb Your Enthusiasm,* Larry's father's friend Solly, a survivor of the death camps, meets Colby Donaldson, a young fellow who had been on the television show *Survivor.* An argument ensues about who had a more difficult time, who suffered more. "But I was in Auschwitz," Solly finally exclaims, after hearing the TV survivor kvetch about having to walk long distances, wear thongs, run out of tasty snacks, and put up with mosquitoes.

Thanks largely to Jewish comics, jokes about the Holocaust and Nazis, for better or worse, have become part of popular culture. Larry David could even joke about the notorious death camp murderer Josef Mengele, the so-called Angel of Death, who was responsible at Auschwitz for the selection of victims to be killed in the gas chambers and who performed deadly human experiments on prisoners. In an old stand-up bit, which ridicules his own vanity, David said, "If he'd given me a compliment, Josef Mengele and I could have been friends— 'Larry, your hair looks very good today.' Really? Thank you, Dr. Mengele!"

What remains off-limits? David, also the co-creator of *Seinfeld*, came up with a character on that series called the Soup Nazi.

Jews feel comfortable enough in America to joke even about Christ in ways that can only be described as over-the-top— such as in the Christmas Day episode of Larry David's *Curb Your Enthusiasm*. Larry thought he was eating animal cookies from a miniature zoo when he actually ate representations from an artificial manger. He discovers, from his Gentile wife, Cheryl, and her family, that he had consumed the baby Jesus and the holy mother Mary.

The past may be prologue, but anxiety about the past and its way of marking Jews is still distinctive. However, popular culture, especially in the United States, has changed the calculus from fear of something appearing too Jewish to Jewish identity that goes often to the other extreme. This can be seen in the contrast between two of the most popular comedy TV shows of all time—*Seinfeld* and *The Jack Benny Show.*

One of America's most popular comedy entertainers, Jack Benny (born Benjamin Kublesky) was an audience favorite in both radio and television from the 1930s to the 1970s. A pioneer of the sitcom, he, along with his wife, Mary Livingstone (née Sadie Marks), became fixtures in the homes of millions of Americans. Like Henny Youngman, his trademark was the violin, but his signature persona was of a lovable skinflint, always and in every way cheap. His Jewishness was never revealed. Rather than being cheap, Benny was actually a generous soul, concocting the cheap Scrooge role for laughs just as he and his good friend Fred Allen made up an ongoing feud between them. When, in 1948, Benny's character was held up and given the option "Your money or your life," he was able to use his brilliant sense of comic timing in what would become his signature skit, saying, after a pause, "I'm thinking! I'm thinking!"

I may be flirting with a thesis here that others will find a stretch. But it has always been striking to me that Benny felt he had to keep his Jewishness entirely under wraps while, a couple of decades later, Jerry Seinfeld would include not only Jewish characters, but a regular lampooning of Jewish themes and stereotypes.

Many Jews, who were well aware of Jack Benny's Jewish identity, believed that the joke underneath the joke, the subtext of much of Benny's humor, was his Jewishness. Yet, with episodes of *The Jack Benny Show* built around Christmas, there was never a hint of anything identifiably Jewish. Nothing! Except perhaps his violin.

It was no secret to Jews all over the world that nearly all of the world's greatest violinists were of Jewish descent. The names continue to rise to the stratosphere of musical achievement—Jascha Heifetz, Yehudi Menuhin, Yitzhak Perlman, and Isaac Stern. Perhaps no other field except medicine (and, of course, comedy) has contained so many stellar figures who were Jewish. Jack Benny, like Henny Youngman, was no master of the instrument, and his violin playing was a kind of inside Jewish joke. The latter never became explicit because Jack Benny, by necessity, remained, alas, closeted as a Jew. To the present day, he can be seen more as an everyman figure, an

American really. That was the aim of Jewish entertainers and writers of all stripes immediately following the Second World War. This is the reason, I believe, why Arthur Miller's Willy Loman in *Death of a Salesman* was never identified as being Jewish. The play appeared in 1949, the year after the your-money-or-your-life *Jack Benny* episode. Though recognizably Jewish, even in idioms and locutions, Willy Loman, created by a Jewish American playwright, remained unidentifiable as a Jew. Young people of today, Jewish or otherwise, would have a hard time detecting any Jewishness either in Jack Benny or Willy Loman. In large part out of the fear of anti-Semitism, concealing Jewishness was deemed necessary so soon after the Holocaust, even, and perhaps particularly, by Jews themselves.

The Jewish executives who green-lighted *Seinfeld,* the popular television show "about nothing," voiced concerns over its being too Jewish. However, Jerry Seinfeld stepped out of the closet and played an openly Jewish character in what was destined to be one of the most successful sitcoms of all time. The creators and most of the writers were Jews, and the New York style of the sitcom gave life to the Lenny Bruce quip that if you were from New York you were Jewish. The character of George was supposed to be only half-Jewish, but both his parents fit the roles of stereotypical Jewish caricatures. Overt Jewish themes were taken on by the writers, including episodes with rabbis, a mohel, and the one about Elaine's "shik-sappeal." There were episodes in which Jerry gets fixed up with a young woman named Donna Chang, who turns out to be a Caucasian Jewish blonde from Long Island whose family name is Changstein. There is Dr. Wattley, Jerry's dentist, who converts to Judaism and feels it gives him license to freely tell Jewish jokes, prompting Jerry, who announces himself a Jew, to inform on the ex-Catholic Wattley to a priest in a confession booth. The priest asks, "Are you offended as a Jew?" and Seinfeld answers, "No. I'm offended as a comedian." We are a long way from Jack Benny.

If you examine nearly any episode of *Seinfeld* having to do overtly with Jews or Jewish identity, you will find ridicule. Which is why, though the relationship of *Seinfeld* to Jews and Jewishness has had many ardent defenders, there are those who insist a number of episodes are self-hating. But, as Woody Allen's character, Harry, in the film *Deconstructing Harry*, said on being called a self-hating Jew: "I may hate myself but not because I'm Jewish."

When I attended a fund-raiser for a PBS Jewish humor documentary, Jerry Stiller (father of Ben and George's father on *Seinfeld*) was emcee. He told a story about the famed Jewish actor Walter Matthau going to visit Auschwitz with his wife. The couple had been fighting the night before and the next morning were still fuming. When the tour ended, Matthau's wife, her eyes streaming with tears, said to her husband, "That puts everything in perspective and ought to make both of us realize how foolish our fighting was." Matthau, according to Jerry Stiller, gave his wife a cold look and said, "It's too late. You ruined Auschwitz for me."

> Two old Jewish men are sitting on a park bench. One looks at the other and says, "Oy." The other looks back and says, "Oy." This is repeated again and again until the first older man says, "I thought we weren't going to talk politics?"

A good joke teller can do marvelous and even brilliant things with just the sounds of "oys" that the printed word cannot equal; but the word alone, "oy," whether uttered or seen on the page, creates a rich stream of associations with kvetching and the suffering of the Jewish past. "Oy" evokes suffering in ways, more than likely, no other two-letter word in any language can. As they say, the journey of a thousand miles begins with a single "oy."

Why is the "oy, vas I thirsty" joke funny? Even when the

old Jew's thirst is quenched, he kvetches about it. The joke is ridiculing a Jewish inability to let go of the past.

A good number of Jewish jokes, like that one, are built on suffering. But in them, too, is a clinging to the idea of sep- arateness, which also can be celebrated. In the diabetes joke, members of every other identity group want liquor except for the Jew. The need and thirst for alcohol may suggest depen- dence, if not addiction, but the joke also tells us Jews are quick to assume the worst. Centuries of suffering can and do breed pessimism.

An old Jew, who prays at the Western Wall, is known to have been going there to pray every day, many times a day, for many years. An enterprising young American reporter is told about the old man and his hours of daily praying. Believing it might make a good human-interest story, the reporter goes to the wall and, sure enough, there is the old man bent in prayer. After watching the old Jew pray for about an hour and a half and then seeing him slowly walk away, cane in hand, the reporter approaches him and asks him his name. The old Jew answers that his name is

Irving Rabinowitz. The reporter then inquires how long Mr. Rabinowitz has been praying at the Western Wall and Rabinowitz answers, "Sixty-seven years."

"That is remarkable," says the young reporter. "What do you pray for?"

Rabinowitz says that he prays for peace between Jews, Muslims, and Christians and for the love of human beings for their fellow humans. He adds that he also prays for politicians to be honest.

At this point, the reporter asks, "So what has it been like for you praying all these years?"

Rabinowitz answers, "It's like talking to a fucking wall."

The joke became quite popular and was even turned into a cartoon. Its meaning is obvious—prayer, even at the Western Wall, is unlikely to be answered, especially if the prayer has anything to do with peace or producing honest politicians. Such prayers have gone unanswered through the millennia. The old man represents the passive Jew who keeps praying even though his response to the reporter is an aggressive one directed at God himself.

The trajectory of a lot of Jewish humor winds up, especially after the Holocaust, with aggression directed at the almighty himself. Lenny Bruce said, "If something about the human body disgusts you, the fault lies with the manufacturer." And recall that Lewis Black called God "a prick." The implication of much of these types of jokes is the question: Where was God when he was really needed? Where was God when Jews were suffering most? Where, too, was his mercy and justice? Yet Jews remain passive and pray. The humor rests in the paradox.

A wonderfully pious and devout Jewish woman, a woman of rectitude and goodness, agrees reluctantly to undergo plastic surgery following her husband's death. She goes along with the urgings of her friends and family to do so, hoping it will provide her with a new beginning, a new lease on life. No sooner does she leave the hospital following her full face-lift than she is struck down by a car and killed. When she meets her Maker in heaven, she does not hesitate to ask God why, given what a good Jew she has been and how many kind and charitable deeds she performed, she had to die so soon and so violently after having just gone under the knife. God shrugs his shoulders and says, "I'm sorry. I didn't recognize you."

This is truly a heretical joke suggesting that an omnipotent and all-seeing God could make a mistake—though an almighty God, the sages might argue, could not be concerned about something as insignificant as plastic surgery or one widow's life. It is also, of course, a joke about the limitations and possible consequences of literally changing faces. But ultimately the woman's piety and devotion are rewarded with meeting God in a heavenly afterlife. Despite the lord's failure to recognize her, the woman is sent to heaven. However, God almighty in the joke may be as susceptible to human error as humans, a chilling thought to believers, but one not so difficult to accept in a post-Auschwitz world.

Two minks are about to be slaughtered.
One mink turns to the other and says, "See you in shul."

The animal jokes, as we have seen, are often akin to Aesop fables. This mink joke, for example, is funny for the obvious reason that many Jewish women were known to dress up for shul (synagogue), especially for High Holiday services. Mink coats were not uncommon for more affluent women to wear in pre-PETA days. But the joke has another layer that is much darker when one thinks, with minks going to the slaughter, of the Holocaust. The joke may be healthy as well as mordant because the minks, though destined to drape the arms and shoulders of Jewish women at shul, nevertheless herald success and prosperity for Jews who have managed to arise, like the phoenix, from the ashes of the Shoah's crematoria and now wear mink coats. Plus they actually attend services!

The Yiddish theater in New York of the late nineteenth and early twentieth century was known as a refuge for the many hardworking Jewish women from the sweatshops. An audience of mainly Jewish women is waiting one night to see the Yiddish Valentino, an iconic actor named Abramowitz, who makes many of the women swoon. The theater owner, Pishocks, steps onto the stage and in solemn and heavy tones delivers the message that the great, magnificent, beloved thespian Abramowitz has died. The audience is stunned. The women are sobbing gut-wrenching sobs. A male voice from up in the balcony shouts, "Give him an enema." Pishocks looks up at the balcony in disbelief. "Are you crazy?" he shouts. "Don't you understand? Abramowitz, the great Abramowitz, is dead! How, in the name of God, could giving him an enema possibly help?" Whereupon we hear back from the balcony the voice shout, "It couldn't hurt."

The joke about the icon Abramowitz dying is not only about the man in the balcony, whose innocence borders on stupidity; the joke also has embedded in it an element of Jewish character that looks for an absurd solution while stubbornly refusing to acknowledge tragedy. In that sense, it evokes the poignancy of a joke like the one about the Jew who is looking to escape Hitler's Germany as the Nazis are rounding up Jews for the slaughter. He goes to a travel agent in Berlin and asks about passage to different parts of the world, only to be told by the agent, who points to a global map, that Jews are not allowed to travel anywhere on the planet. No country is accepting them. The Jew then asks the travel agent, "Perhaps you could show me a different globe?"

Then there is the joke about the Jew reading *Der Stürmer*, the hateful Nazi paper. A friend and fellow Jew cannot understand why he reads such evil propaganda and asks, "Why are you reading that odious paper *Der Stürmer*?" The Jew answers, "I read the regular Jewish papers about pogroms, assimilation, riots in Palestine, and then I read *Der Stürmer* about how we

Jews control politics and are taking over the world, and I feel much better."

Do such jokes resonate in today's world? Do they resonate to Jewish American youth like the kids at my synagogue who drew portraits of Abraham alongside those of Steven Spielberg? Perhaps. But mostly they throw us back to another time and place. And yet they seem, also, to reveal to us, like the enema joke, something believed to be elemental about Jews and suffering.

Though anti-Semitism obviously continues to live in America, and is once again escalating across the globe, a document from the Warsaw ghetto had in it (in Yiddish) a tragically funny line. The line speaks to Jewish survival in the face of adversity, even horror. It was written before the Shoah ended, but is as relevant today as it was then: "God forbid that this war should last as long as we are able to endure it."

There are a number of so-called Holocaust jokes, many out of Europe, obviously forged in bigotry. Alan Dundes, the folklorist and anthropology professor at UC Berkeley, who was known as Professor Joke because of his widely popular classes on humor, helped bring them to public attention. Like the one about the ashes of exterminated Jews in ashtrays of German-made Volkswagens. Or the one about asking a Jewish woman for her number by telling her to roll up her sleeve. Or the reason Hitler fainted? He saw his gas bill. Or yet another hideous one asking what the difference is between a Jew and a pizza. Pizzas don't scream. Jokes like those, if one can even grace them with the word "joke," are more apt to be heard among hate groups or told by genuine anti-Semites or seen on neo-Nazi websites.

When *The Producers* first appeared in 1968, its famous song-and-dance routine, "Springtime for Hitler," which joked about the Nazi führer and Germany's master race, caused a furor. Many were taken aback at the perceived bad taste of using swastikas, Heil Hitlers, and a storm trooper goose-stepping set to a Busby Berkeley–style musical number. Of course Mel Brooks, like Charlie Chaplin before him in *The Little Dictator*, was not only poking fun at Hitler and Nazis—he was satirizing Broadway producers, his two being Max Bialystock and Leo Bloom, and their attempt to produce a surefire failure in order to get out of debt.

It is the early 1980s and a young, enterprising German reporter working out of Buenos Aires is told that Hitler, though in his nineties, is still very much alive. Moreover, the reporter is informed, the führer can be seen going into diatribes once a week in an Argentine

rathskeller where a few of his old Nazi comrades con-
gregate and continue to feed on his every word. The
reporter's informant, a distant relative of his among
the group of old Nazis, tells him he will let him know
when Hitler will next be in the rathskeller.

When the time comes, the reporter manages to
slip in to see, in utter disbelief, a number of old Ger-
mans toasting and adoring a little old man who is
immediately recognized by the reporter, even after
much aging and a decidedly morphed appearance, as
the once leader of the Third Reich.

The timbre of his voice and his gestures, though
ragged and timeworn, are clearly and unmistakably
those of the Nazi führer.

Hitler is speaking with age-ravaged histrionic
fury to the small claque of old ex-Nazis about how
all Jews must be exterminated and, he adds, all acro-
bats. He bangs his fist on the table in front of him and
bellows, in German, in an old and cracked voice, "If
Germany is to rise again as our fatherland is destined
to do, we must eliminate all the Jews, every single
one of them, and each and every one of the acrobats."

The young German reporter is mesmerized and
nearly numb in disbelief. It really is Hitler! What a

story! What an exclusive for him! He cannot contain his feelings of good fortune, knowing that his career as a journalist is now assured. But he also cannot contain his curiosity. He shouts out in German to Hitler, "Why the acrobats?" Without hesitation, Hitler points to him and shouts out to all, in German, "I told you, no one gives a fuck about the Jews."

Is this too out of bounds for humor? Should the subject of the Shoah and, by association, all that the Nazis viciously perpetrated, be off-limits for jokes? These were bigger questions back when *The Producers* first appeared, but they endure. Is it good or bad for the Jews?

Though jokes that seem ill-spirited often are, the reception of many Jewish jokes on sensitive or touchy subjects depends on who tells and who hears them. You be the judge. But please bear in mind what a boyhood friend of mine's uncle Meyer said while eating a lot of greasy, schmaltz-(chicken-fat-) laden Jewish food. Uncle Meyer looked up from his dish of schmaltz herring and said, "Schmaltz may have killed more Jews than Hitler." This is also the kind of food that prompted me once on air to tell food journalist guru Michael Pollan that he was fooling himself by saying we all need to eat simple, healthy diets like our grandparents and great-grandparents. "Are you kidding?" I said to

Pollan. "You're an Ashkenazi Jew! Your grandparents and great-grandparents probably ate tons of schmaltz and greasy, high-cholesterol food. You think with all that *gribenes* and schmaltz and fatty brisket, they weren't clogging their arteries?"

It is Yom Kippur, the holiest and most sacred day in the Jewish calendar. The synagogue is full. A Jewish man tries to enter the sanctuary but is told by the *shammash* (sexton) that it is forbidden to enter without a ticket. The man pleads with the sexton that it is vital for him to speak to his business associate Eli Ratner. The *shammash* shakes his head. "I'm sorry," he says. "I cannot let you in without a ticket." The man says, "I just need twenty seconds. No more. I have to tell Eli Ratner something that is vital and cannot wait. Please let me in. It will be a mitzvah if you do. I promise I will be in there for only twenty seconds, not a second more."

"Okay," says the *shammash*. "But you have to also promise me you won't pray."

Yom Kippur is the day to atone for all sins, to suffer for them really, which Lewis Black says is the main thing he's carried with him from his Jewish upbringing. As a kid, Black said, Yom Kippur had a profound effect on his innocent mind, especially with the organ playing "Kol Nidre," which he called one of the spookiest pieces of music ever written. He added that when you hear it, you are surprised "bats and shit aren't flying around."

Millions of Jews still worship and pray in ways that go back hundreds, even thousands, of years. But with a few notable exceptions, and for better or worse, modern synagogues, like Jewish philanthropic organizations, have taken on ways that are far from European and diasporic roots. Despite their needing a ticket to pray, the value of praying to God and seeking forgiveness on the highest holy day remains inseparable, for many observant and even nonobservant Jews, from a day of fasting and serious lamenting one's transgressions.

And yet, like Lewis Black, many Jews continue to carry a burden of suffering, and it is expressed not only on Yom Kippur but every other day as well. Think of the great neurotic Jewish comics—Woody Allen, Buddy Hackett, Joan Rivers, Larry David, Howard Stern. Also Richard Lewis, who went pacing around the stage like a caged animal and built a career out of saying he was in pain. His actual alcoholism revealed that he wasn't entirely joking. He spoke once on the Letterman show of going off to a place in Santa Barbara for psychological relief called Wounded Jew.

Now, that is funny! And funny, as many of the great Jewish comics have demonstrated over and over through the years, beats the hell out of suffering.

VII.

Separate & Distinct

When John Paul, the Polish pope, was pontiff, there was a joke about him calling a fellow Pole in to get an estimate on a job to decorate a room in the Vatican. After measuring and assessing the room, the Polish decorator says he'll do the job for $3,000. The pope asks for a breakdown of the estimate and the Polish decorator tells him, "One thousand for labor. One thousand for materials. And one thousand for me." The pope says he will need to get additional estimates. He brings in an Italian decorator, who goes through the same measuring and assessing and says he will do the job for $6,000. The pontiff asks the Italian decorator for a breakdown of the costs and the Italian decorator says, "Two thousand for labor. Two thousand for materials. And two thousand for me." Finally, the pope brings in a Jewish decorator, who says to him, straight out, "I will do the job for nine thousand dollars." The pope asks the Jewish decorator for the cost breakdown and the Jewish decorator says, "Three thousand for you, three thousand for me, and three thousand for the Polish decorator."

A wealthy Jewish couple go to the UK to find themselves a high-toned British butler. They find the most elegant one in the entire British Isles and bring him home to their spacious, affluent home in the U.S. suburbs. An anglophile's dream of a butler named Edwin, he is now in their employ, living in their home, and serving them. His first Sunday on the job, they tell him they are having friends over named Silverman, and they would like for him to set the table for four while they go out for their regular Sunday walk. When they return home they see that the table is beautifully set for eight. They are puzzled by this and the husband asks the butler: "Edwin. We told you the Silvermans were coming and asked you to set the table for the four of us. Why is the table set for eight?" Edwin answers, "Sir. The Silvermans called while you were on your walk and said they were bringing the bagels and the bialys."

T HE OLD line about the key to success, "Dress British. Think Yiddish," gives sartorial props to the Brits but features Jews as being the smart tribe, the ones with Yiddish *kops*. Another old joke tells us that the difference between the British (one can easily substitute Gentiles or WASPs) is that Brits leave without saying good-bye while Jews say good-bye without leaving. Jokes of this kind separate Jews from "the other," whoever or whatever the other might be. Even a quick, silly joke, one that asks the question why the bee wore a yarmulke. *The bee wore a yarmulke, of course, so it wouldn't be mistaken for a WASP.*

There was, a while back, a whole subgenre of jokes described as WASP jokes, essentially about perceived Jewish differences from WASPs:

A WASP calls his parents and tells them he is sorry but he won't be able to fly out to visit them on the weekend as promised. Their response: "Fine."

A WASP sees another WASP on the street and asks, "How's business?" The second WASP says, "Fine."

A WASP sees a suit in a clothing store window on sale for $469. He goes into the store and asks the salesman if the price is the same as the one in the window and the salesman tells the WASP there is no sale. The WASP says, "Fine."

Many of the jokes involving comparisons between Jews and those of other backgrounds serve, as we have seen, to highlight Jewish difference, often Jewish superiority. But the question arises, if Jews feel superior to others, why do so many have inferiority complexes?

The subgenre described as WASP jokes really involves Jewish jokes in disguise. Such jokes distinguish a separate identity for Jews based on timeworn stereotypes about Jews having overly possessive parents, kvetching about business, and looking for lower prices.

Is the joke about the Vatican contractors anti-Polish? Yes. Though the Pole in the joke can be viewed as the most honest of the three decorators, the joke creates a hierarchy based on stereotyping. The joke also has a strange albeit twisted chauvinistic pride in the Jew being more cunning and manipulative about money, which is often celebrated—despite its being at the root of much anti-Semitism.

Let's, again, go back to Jackie Mason and imagine his inflected and unique voice with its distinct cadences saying, "I know a guy. He's half-Jewish and half-Italian. If he can't get something wholesale, he steals it." Or, "I know a guy. He's half-Polish and half-Jewish. He's a janitor. But he owns the building." Mason, in effect, elevates Jews and the Yiddish *kop*, by using stereotypes of Italians being crooks and Poles being janitors, just as the WASP jokes elevate Jews by portraying WASPs as unflappable compared to Jews, far less emotional, warm, or enterprising, though also not as neurotic.

Mason made use of a barrage of stereotypes—even angering my sweet friend Rita Moreno by saying he went to Puerto Rico every year to visit his hubcaps. He built a career on Jew-versus-Gentile jokes . . . for example, Gentiles want the key to the toilet in the workplace while Jews want the key to the vault. Or Gentiles live in homes full of tools that make their homes look like a workshop, while Jews own fancy, expensive art pieces that make their homes look like museums. Jackie Mason made use of the same type of over-the-top stereotyping shtick with Jewish men and black men.

The sad fact is, many Jewish jokes have prejudiced or bigoted views embedded in them, where Jewish chosenness is highlighted, often at the expense of another group—or other groups, as we plainly see in a good deal of Jackie Mason's shtick. Lenny Bruce had a famous bit that I mentioned a while back called "Jewish and Goyish," in which he went through a whole list of differences, including the famous: "If you live in New York or any other big city, you are Jewish. It doesn't matter even if you're Catholic; if you live in New York, you're Jewish. If you live in Butte, Montana, you're going to be goyish even if you're Jewish." In other words, being Jewish means being cosmopolitan rather than provincial, which means goyish.

Larry David's character in *Curb Your Enthusiasm* discovers, and for a while believes, he was adopted and is really of Christian ancestry, and as a result everything, especially in his character, is altered. He becomes, in effect, nice, passive, forgiving, generous, and unassuming. In other words, he becomes, with Jewish stereotypes in mind, the WASP anti-Jew.

Jews in jokes who try to act like Gentiles invariably give themselves away, as in the joke set in London in an upscale new deli. An older Jewish lady enters and asks the man behind the counter for a pound of lox and is told (use snobby British accent here): "Madam, please, we call it Nova Scotia." Then she tells him she wants blintzes, and the snobby British counter guy tells her to please only refer to them as crêpes. Finally, she asks for a pound of chopped liver, and once more he rebukes her and tells her she must say pâté. So the older Jewish lady orders a pound of Nova Scotia, five crêpes, and a pound of pâté and asks that it all be delivered to her home on Saturday morning. Whereupon, the seemingly highbred, snobbish counterman says, "But, if you please, madam, we never schlep on Shabbos."

So what makes a Jewish joke other than the fact that it may have Yiddish words or locutions or Jewish content? There are, after all, certain jokes told about Jews that easily translate to other ethnicities or even professions. When I was a kid, I couldn't get over how often Jews were compared to Italians. Both, I kept hearing, put great emphasis on family, food, tradition, and education. But I heard the identical thing said about Jews and Chinese. I remember hearing those analogies repeatedly over the course of my life, and I've wondered why I never hear Italians compared to Chinese or Chinese to Italians.

There is the joke that asks what Jewish Alzheimer's is. The answer: "You forget everything but the grudges." (Another version substitutes guilt for grudges.) A good joke for Jews, perhaps, but I've heard Italians (especially Sicilians), Irish, and Arabs used by others telling that same joke.

Usually I try to shy away from being too ethnocentric on

the radio, but I wanted to interview Ruth R. Wisse, Harvard professor of Yiddish and comparative literature, about her book *No Joke: Making Jewish Humor*. We cracked a few Jewish jokes during the interview and I wasn't surprised when emails, postings, and tweets followed suggesting that some of the jokes were applicable to certain other cultures, or were even universal. "Jews have no premium on a number of the jokes you told," one indignant emailer wrote. Well, perhaps. At least perhaps for some of them. And, regardless, good humor indeed is, or ought to be, universal. My friend the novelist Isabel Allende swears that the humor from her native Chile is in every way just like Jewish humor.

My wife and I spent an evening with Amy Tan and her husband, Lou, at their home a few years ago, and I was interested to hear Amy offer a joke to me about a doctor, a lawyer, and a Chinese man getting haircuts. They each had their hair cut on different days from a barber who insisted that, since it was their first haircut from him, they not pay. The barber found a gift outside his shop from the doctor the day after and another outside his shop from the lawyer after he cut the lawyer's hair. The day after he cut the Chinese man's hair, there were dozens of Chinese men outside his barbershop. What interested me about this joke, of course, was that it had been told, when I first heard it and many times after, about a minister, a priest, and a rabbi.

The fact is, jokes often morph and take on different cultural identities regardless of the identity in the original version. Yet some jokes remain inescapably Jewish. There's a famous joke that has always struck me somehow as a Jewish joke, though I have never been able to determine or pin down exactly why this is so. It somehow just is. It is the one about the man who walks into a restaurant and orders soup.

After the waiter sets the bowl down on the table, the man asks him to try the soup, and the waiter says, "Is it too hot?" The man says, "No, just try the soup." The waiter says, "Is it too cold?" Again, the man says no and repeats himself, "Just try the soup, please."

The waiter then asks, "Does it need more seasoning?"

The man shakes his head and says once more, "No, no, just try my soup."

The waiter finally agrees and says, "Where's the spoon?"

The man says, "Aha!"

So how do we determine a uniquely Jewish joke that won't or can't cross over?

An example of a Jewish joke that cannot possibly migrate is a well-known, sweet one, set once again across the pond in Britain.

A brilliant, religious Jewish man named Feinberg is to be knighted by the queen of England for his discoveries and achievements as a leading scientific researcher. A number of men, including Feinberg, kneel before the queen in order to be knighted. After going from one to the other, she comes upon Feinberg and cannot help but notice that he is wearing a yarmulke. Which causes her to ask, "Why is this knight different from all other knights?"

This reminds me of the joke about young Henry, who is asked by his father to say the evening prayer and realizes he doesn't have his head covered. He asks his brother, Korey, to rest a hand on his head until the prayers are over. Korey grows impatient after a few minutes and removes his hand.

The father says, "This is important . . . put your hand back on your brother's head!" To which Korey says, "Am I my brother's *kippah?*"

A Japanese emperor in ancient Japan puts out a proclamation seeking a chief samurai. A Japanese, Chinese, and Jewish samurai all apply and the emperor orders each to demonstrate his samurai skills. The Japanese samurai immediately steps forward, opens a tiny box, and releases a fly. He draws his samurai sword and *SWISH,* he neatly divides the fly into two.

"What skill!" exclaims the emperor.

Then the Chinese samurai steps forward, opens a tiny box, releases a fly, draws his samurai sword, and *SWISH SWISH,* the fly falls to the floor neatly quartered.

"That is very skillful!" shouts the emperor.

Then comes the Jewish samurai, who also opens a tiny box and releases a fly, draws his samurai sword, and *SWOOOOSH,* brings forth a huge gust of wind that blows through the room. But the fly continues to buzz around. The emperor says, "Where is your skill? The fly is not even dead."

"Dead?" replies the Jewish samurai. "Dead is easy. Circumcision—now, that takes skill!"

This is yet another joke about Jewish superiority. The Jewish samurai is a remarkably able amateur mohel, the person who performs ritual circumcisions. (Old joke: *A British mohel who "took tips" was knighted as Sir Cumsized.*)

It is striking how often Jews and the Japanese connect in Jewish jokes. Following the end of World War II and the defeat of Japan by Allied forces, there were many Japanese who had practiced Shintoism, the religion of Emperor Hirohito, who ultimately converted to Judaism. This prompted me, when I first read about it as a kid, to ask if we were going to start hearing Japanese people saying "shalom" rather than "sayonara."

A dignified-looking Japanese gentleman, complete with top hat and walking stick, goes up to a Jewish woman in Manhattan and asks if she can tell him the best way to find the library. She looks him up and down, then says, "Pearl Harbor you could find, but you can't find the library?"

A man is half-Jewish and half-Japanese. Every December 7, he attacks Pearl Schwartz.

A new Jewish Japanese restaurant opens. It's called So Sue Me.

Even these three jokes insist on Jewish difference via stereotype—the tough, unforgiving New York Jewish woman, the aggressively sexual Jew, and the litigious Jew. Such jokes have their own special cultural provenance.

A Jewish deli guy sees an Arab walk in, an obvious sheikh, complete with robe and headdress. The Arab asks for twenty corned beef sandwiches, and the deli guy whispers to his boss, "There's an Arab who wants twenty corned beef sandwiches. What should I do?" His boss quickly responds: "Tell him they're twenty bucks apiece." The counter guy makes the sandwiches, charges the Arab twenty bucks for each, and the Arab pays in cash. The next day the Arab returns and asks for sixty corned beef sandwiches. The counter guy whispers to his boss, who quickly says, "Tell him they cost sixty bucks per sandwich." Again, the counter guy repeats the price and gets paid in cash. The next day the same exact thing occurs but the Arab asks for and receives a hundred corned beef sandwiches at a hundred dollars each. The following day a sign goes up on the deli reading: NO JEWS ALLOWED.

How would you read that joke? Jews being willing to exclude their own to meet an increasingly lucrative opportunity? Do Jews feel comfortable laughing at that joke since it does, in effect, also mean they are enterprising, pragmatic, and shrewd? Or is it too moored in the discomfort and bad taste of stereotyping Jews as money-grubbers? Or does the basic premise of an Arab buying corned beef sandwiches in a Jewish deli make it an all-too-obvious-not-to-be-taken-serious joke from the get-go?

An Arab is nearly dying of thirst trying to cross the desert when he comes across a Jew who, there in the middle of the desert, is selling ties. The Arab is furious with the Jew, who is high-pressuring him to purchase one of the ties he has on display. "Can't you see I'm dying of thirst?" the Arab screams. "You lower-than-a-rat Jew. Have you no mercy?" The tie-selling Jew then informs the Arab that over the next small sand dune a few miles ahead is a new, air-conditioned restaurant where the Arab can get all the water he wants or needs. The Arab crawls and barely makes it over the sand dune only to return hours later gasping and obviously about to die of thirst. The Jew asks him what happened. The Arab's last words, barely audible: "They wouldn't let me in without a tie."

Years after I first heard that particular joke, I heard it repeated in a version in which a man from the Taliban crawling across a desert in Afghanistan meets up with the Jewish tie salesman. Either way, it is the Jew who is the enterprising one, even in the desert, which for decades Jews in Israel have said they (like Bugsy Siegel in Las Vegas) caused to bloom.

Another joke comes swiftly to mind, related to me by Bob Simon, the well-known Jewish CBS and *60 Minutes* television correspondent who was tragically killed in a car crash on the West Side Highway in New York City. The joke takes place during the time when what came to be called "the troubles" were going on in Northern Ireland. In fact, Simon, who was on assignment, was beaten during that time by Protestant Irish thugs. Nevertheless, he savored telling me the joke about a neophyte Jewish newsman assigned to Belfast during those troubled times.

A stranger comes up behind a Jewish newsman in Belfast, shoves a gun into his back, and demands, "Protestant or Catholic?" Knowing his life is at stake and not knowing if the man holding the gun is a Protestant or a Catholic, the Jewish newsman elects to tell the truth. "I am neither," he says. "I am a Jew." He hears the man with the gun cackling with laughter, then hears him say, "I must be the luckiest Arab in Belfast."

Simon's joke also brings to mind a young Irish Catholic man I know who fell in love with a young Jewish woman. His mother, who was born in Belfast, was a devout Catholic. When he told her he had fallen in love with a Jewish girl, she paused, pursed her lips in a bit of a scowl, then said, "Well, at least she's not Protestant."

Which leads to an anecdote about an Irish Catholic male and a Jewish female. My wife and I are in a small apartment in Berkeley where my wife's older female cousin and her daughter are in the kitchen cutting vegetables. My wife and I are in the adjacent living room sitting on a couch listening to the daughter's Irish boyfriend detailing to us, with relish, how he and the daughter run three miles every morning, get an endorphin high, then return to the apartment and have "incredible, remarkable, fantastic, hot sex." No sooner do those words tumble from his mouth than the mother sticks her head out from the kitchen like a pop-up puppet and shouts, "So who needs to know this?"

Question: Why don't Jews like living in the wilderness?

Answer: No running water, no electricity, no hot and sour soup.

Philip Roth, in his novel *Operation Shylock*, repeats the by-now-famous joke about the Chinese waiter working in a delicatessen who speaks astonishingly good Yiddish. A customer overhears him and says to the deli owner: "That waiter of yours really speaks damn good Yiddish." The owner quickly puts his finger across his lips and shushes the man, saying, "Shhhh. He thinks he's learning English."

Where the Chinese are concerned, there is often humor tied to how much Jews love Chinese food.

A friend of mine, who is Jewish, announced at a dinner party that his son was set to marry a young woman from China. "I'm sorry," an older Jewish woman who was seated with us at the dinner table responded. Then she added, "Intermarriage is hard enough, but interracial marriage, that's much much harder." There was silence and a palpable sense of discomfort until my friend said, "It could be worse. My son could be marrying someone Orthodox."

(A famous joke about a man stranded on an island for decades highlights the theme of divisiveness among Jews. Over the course of time he builds two temples. When he is rescued and asked why he went to the trouble of building two separate temples, he points to one and says, "I would never worship at that one.")

Then there is the story of a tourist in San Francisco who sees a sign on an establishment that says MOISHE PLOTNICK'S CHINESE LAUNDRY. He is intrigued (as I have said, I am about why the name Plotnick surfaces in a number of Jewish jokes), so he enters the establishment and sees a Chinese man behind the counter. Immediately he asks him, "If you don't mind my asking, how did this Chinese laundry get the name Moishe Plotnik?" In a thick Chinese accent, the man behind the counter says that he is Moishe Plotnik. The tourist is shocked. "You are Moishe Plotnik? How can that be? Moishe Plotnik is a Jewish name!" The Chinese owner smiles and, in broken English, tells how he went through immigration into the United States behind a man named Moishe Plotnik. When asked his name by the immigration officer in charge, he said, "Sam Ting."

A Jew and a Catholic are in Mexico City soliciting charitable contributions from passersby. They stand apart by about thirty yards and each holds out to those walking by a small collection barrel for donations. The Catholic has a crucifix above his collection barrel, the Jew a Star of David. A nicely dressed American goes up to the Jew and says to him, "It's none of my business, but as you no doubt can see, the fellow with the crucifix is getting all the money put in his collection barrel while you are getting none. Is it any wonder? Mexico is a Catholic country. Perhaps you should consider a better place." The Jew gives the man a blank stare and then shouts down to the man with the crucifix: "Hey, Muttel, this guy is telling us how we should do our business!"

Here are a couple of smart Jews conning Mexicans. The vexing question of whether the joke is anti-Semitic, again, has to do perhaps more with who is telling it. But the essence of the joke, which could substitute nearly any other Christian country in place of Mexico, is the stereotypic view of cunning, moneymaking Jews.

A priest, a minister, and a rabbi, all friends, decide together to purchase new cars. The priest and the minister baptize their new cars, while the rabbi takes a hacksaw to his and cuts three inches off the tailpipe.

There are a bevy of jokes that feature a priest, a minister, and a rabbi, most revealing Jewish distinctiveness.

A priest, a minister, and a rabbi are discussing when conception takes place. The priest says, "At conception." The minister says, "When the fetus is viable or out of the mother's womb." The rabbi says, "When the kids graduate from college and the dog dies."

A rabbi and a priest are in a plane about to crash. The rabbi grabs a parachute, while the priest, by mistake, takes the rabbi's tallis bag.

A rabbi and a priest get into a car accident and cannot agree on who is at fault. The rabbi amicably offers the priest some of his kiddush wine while the two try to come to a decision about who bears responsibility. The rabbi keeps offering more and more kiddush wine to the priest as the pair chat amicably. The rabbi does not drink, but when the priest is intoxicated, the rabbi informs him that he has called the police to come make an accident report.

Given the long history, going back to the Inquisition, or earlier, of Catholic persecution of Jews, most of the rabbi-priest jokes have the rabbi as a stand-in for all Jews outwitting or outsmarting a priest, a stand-in for all Roman Catholics.

There is a great old Yiddish figure of speech that parallels the well-known English one of a bull in a china shop. The analogous words in Yiddish translate to a Cossack in a sukkah. But the joke about the rabbi plying the priest with wine may also be a form of payback, a revenge fantasy for the inglorious past of Jewish persecution at the hands of priests and their minions.

You can see how these jokes separate and distinguish Jew from Catholic. Nevertheless, each of the jokes establishes something else—which is fraternization. Regardless of who comes out on top, the Jew and the Catholic are now talking to each other and have, at least as the jokes are framed, put behind roles of victim and victimizer for interfaith mingling.

It is a dreadful Russian winter, as unbearably cold and freezing as we find in Gogol's St. Petersburg–set classic story "The Overcoat." A crowd of Russians waits for an hour in long lines in the terrible winter until an official tells them that there is less meat than expected and all Jews must leave and return to their homes. Another hour goes by and snow is coming down hard, and the same official announces that even less meat will arrive and therefore all who are not Communists must leave and return to their homes. Then, ultimately, those remaining are told there is no meat at all and they, too, will need to return to their homes. As a couple of the Communists head on home, one of them says to the other, "The Jews always get to go home first."

This is another one of those Jews-can't-win jokes—but it is one set in a specific time—in Russia when a great deal of attention was being paid to the plight of Soviet Jews and Cold War anti-communism was strong. These kinds of jokes lasted for years, especially prior to perestroika and glasnost. There was, in fact, a Russian Jewish comedian named Yakov Smirnoff who, invoking Henny Youngman's classic "take my wife, please" joke, pointed out that if he told that same joke in Russia, he might have come home to find his wife not there.

When I interviewed Vladimir Posner, one of the leading journalists in the then Soviet Union, I told him a joke on air that was set in contemporary Russia. Thanks largely to Ted Koppel and Phil Donahue, Posner became a celebrity in the United States, mainly as a Soviet propagandist engaged in what were hyped as Cold War issue-oriented debates and town meetings. Posner had a Jewish father and was a product of Stuyvesant High School in Manhattan; he was a smart, deft, and fluent speaker of English. I was with ABC at the time. I told him the joke on air, fearing he might be offended and balk at it, but it caused him to laugh hard and sparked a curious discussion between us about the plight of Jews in Russia.

A Jewish man with a pencil and a small tablet of paper is in a Russian supermarket. He goes over to the meat counter, sees no meat, and writes down on the paper, in capital letters, "NO MEAT." Then he goes over to where the fish are supposed to be displayed, but there is only one piece of a somewhat frail-and rotten-looking fish. He writes down "ONE FISH." A Russian officer of the law walks up to the Jew and belligerently asks him, "What do you think you are doing, Comrade?" The Jew nervously responds that he simply is taking stock of what is available in the supermarket and writing it all down as a personal inventory. The official grimaces, then says, "You realize, Comrade, that just a few years ago you could have been shot for what you are doing?" The Jew nods his head, then marks down "NO BULLETS."

Jews have never had it easy in Russia. My paternal grandfather, who emigrated from that country, used to note that the Jews in Russia for centuries would say, "This czar is bad enough. Who needs a new one?"

There is a funny story, a kind of Conan Doyle tale of Talmudic reasoning, that takes us back to czarist Russia and reveals the constraints Jews were put under but also shows the close-knit nature of Jewish lives and communities and the ratiocinative powers of a Talmudic scholar.

The tale begins in Odessa with a Talmudic scholar who must go through long and tense negotiations with the authorities in order simply to be allowed to travel by train to Moscow. He is on board the train and it comes to a stop. The Talmudic scholar sees a young man board the train and the young man sits down across from him. The Talmudist can tell by the young man's bearing that he is not a peasant and therefore must come from the district where he got on the train, which happens to be a Jewish district, and therefore the young man must be a Jew.

The Talmudist begins to wonder. If the young man is a Jew, where is he going? He, the Talmud scholar, is the only Jew in his district with permission to travel to Moscow. But, he thinks, outside of Moscow is a small village called Vlestok and Jews do not need to have permission to travel there. So the young man must be going to Vlestok and therefore why is he going there? No doubt to visit one of the Jewish families who live in the village! The Talmudist continues to reason that only two Jewish families, the Steingarts and the Friedmans, reside in the village, and the Friedmans are dreadful people. The handsome and respectable-looking young man must therefore be going to visit the Steingarts!

More reasoning proceeds in the Talmudist's mind. The Steingarts have only two daughters, Rebecca and Rachel. Perhaps the young man is a son-in-law? But of which daughter would he be the husband? Rebecca Steingart, he had heard, was married to a nice lawyer from Budapest, while Rachel Steingart married a businessman from another village. So the young man must be Rebecca's husband. Which means, the Talmudist thinks to himself, "His name, if I am not mistaken, is Alexander Cohen." The scholar continues to reason that if the young man is from Budapest, he must have changed his name because of the rabid anti-Semitism there. The Hungarian equivalent of Cohen, he thinks, is Kovács. If he was granted permission to change his name, the Talmudic scholar deduces, he must have special status. "It must be a university doctorate," he reasons. "It could be nothing less."

At this point the Talmud scholar turns to the young man and says, "Excuse me. Do you mind if I open the window, Dr. Kovács?"

"No," says the startled young man. "But how did you know my name?"

"It was obvious," said the Talmudist.

The leaders of the United States, Russia, and Israel are drawn together to meet with God and are personally informed by God that the world will come to an end in twenty-four hours. The president of the United States goes on national television and tells his fellow American citizens that, yes, the world will end, but they can take comfort in knowing God exists because, like Moses, he, the president, spoke directly with him. The head of Russia tells his fellow Russians to prepare for the end and also informs them that, contrary to Marxist teaching and Communist dogma, God really does, in fact, exist because he, the Russian leader, learned of the impending doom from God himself. Finally, the Israeli head of state goes on television and announces to all of his nation's citizenry, "I spoke to God directly. And guess what he told me? In twenty-four hours no more Palestinian problem!"

Israeli humor is different and is its own brand—often political. The humorist Ephraim Kishon drew upon what he highlighted as Israel's "differentness" from the rest of the world. There is a whole catalog of Kishon statements to that effect.

Israel is the only country in the world, according to Kishon, where patients give doctors advice, taxi drivers read Spinoza and Maimonides, and small talk is defined as a loud and angry debate over politics.

Israel, Kishon wrote, is the only country where the ultra-Orthodox beat up the police rather than the other way around, or where the people are surrounded on all sides by enemies but their headaches are caused by their neighbors upstairs.

Golda Meir, the former prime minister of Israel, had a wonderful sense of humor. When Henry Kissinger, then the U.S. secretary of state, declared that he was first an American, second secretary of state, and third a Jew, Golda Meir supposedly responded to him by saying, "That's fine, Henry. But in

Hebrew everything is written from right to left." Also, when the then U.S. president Richard Nixon allegedly told Golda Meir that both his secretary of state, the German-born Henry Kissinger, and her foreign affairs minister, British-born Abba Eban, were Jewish, she said, "Yes. But mine is the only one who speaks proper English."

A frog and a scorpion meet on the banks of the Jordan River. Both want to get over to the other side. The scorpion says to the frog, "I bet if we work together we can make it across." The frog appears dubious. "You would just sting me and I would die." "No! No!" says the scorpion. "If I sting you, I, too, will immediately die. Why would I do that? There is no reason!" So the frog reluctantly agrees. The scorpion gets onto the frog's back and the two move forward with real progress as all of the frog's four legs and the scorpion's eight propel them through the rushing waters of the Jordan. When they are about halfway across, the scorpion stings the frog and both are suddenly dying. "Why?" moans the frog. "Why did you sting me knowing it would kill both of us? Why?" As he is dying the scorpion says, "Because. This is the Middle East."

I have always assumed that story came from Israelis who saw themselves as the frog more than the scorpion. Except Arabs, as well as Israelis more critical of their own government, would likely view Israel as the scorpion. The story had more currency in Israel and suggests, from an Israeli point of view, how tenuous and impossible peace, especially lasting peace, seems to be in the region. It demonstrates specifically, once again, with grim humor, how peace is seemingly impossible between Israeli and Arab, and obviously has a distinctly Israeli feel and sensibility.

I went to Israel for the first time on a Koret Fellowship in 1994. On my way from Ben Gurion Airport to Jerusalem I asked my wife if she thought perhaps I might have some sort of a mystical experience in the Holy Land. After all, this was the land of Abraham, the land supposedly granted by God to his people. But beyond that, Jerusalem was the city where mystical forces from the ancient Jewish past were said to operate and divine mysteries revealed. People of all faiths have been afflicted by what has come to be called the Jerusalem syndrome, a mystical-like experience, often viewed as a form of madness, induced simply by being in the holy city. I told friends before I went, "If I am ever to have a mystical experience, it seems it will happen in Israel, most likely in Jerusalem."

The car we were in stopped and the two of us got out on Ben Yehuda Street. No sooner had I stepped onto the street than I spotted him standing only a few feet from me. It felt like nothing short of an hallucination to see him there, literally right in front of me. We shook hands, and I said to him, "I was wondering if I would have a mystical experience in Israel, and here you are, the first person I see as I step onto the soil of Eretz Yisrael in Jerusalem. Do you perhaps still think you are the Jew's Messiah?" He laughed and my wife and I proceeded on our way. When I returned home, friends were eager to know if I had had a mystical experience. "No," I told them. "But as soon as I stepped onto a street in Jerusalem, I ran into Alan Dershowitz."

A Jew, a Frenchman, and a Russian are stranded on a small island with sharks swimming all around and no other land in sight. Nor is there any food to eat or water to drink. After days pass, the agitated Frenchman, who envisions his end, howls at their fate. The Russian joins him with shouts of despair. The Jew? He tells the other two he has no worries. He is absolutely certain he will be found. "How can you be sure?" asks the Frenchman. "Yes," echoes the Russian. "How can you say that?" The Jew says: "I made a pledge to the United Jewish Appeal. They'll find me"

The implication of the joke, of course, is that Jewish charitable organizations will track down anyone who has pledged money. This, indeed, speaks volumes about the tenacity and resourcefulness of organized Jewish philanthropy. As a teen growing up in Cleveland, I was appalled at a tactic the Jewish Welfare Federation used one year to make sure those who did not meet their pledges were shamed. They printed a book listing amounts of money pledged and amounts actually received or not received.

Jewish children learn the value of *tzedakah* early, putting coins in blue boxes from the Jewish National Fund marked *"keren ami,"* or participating in a range of synagogue-run charitable drives and activities.

A teacher asks three children in the classroom, including a Jewish boy named Jonathan, to state their name, age, and hobby.

"I'm Petra. I'm nine. I like to roller-skate."
"I'm Jimmy. I'm ten. I collect coins."
"I'm Jonathan. I'm ten. I pledge."

Jokes like these present Jews as having distinct and separate identities from others, extending back even to childhood.

A Chabadnik who lives in Massachusetts goes on a mission from his Chabad house in Boston to set up a Chabad house in the Deep South. He goes by train to Mississippi, where the hope is that he will serve communities of Jews and spread the Chabad message of Torah and traditional Judaism. The train takes him first to Memphis, where he waits in the station for another train that will take him to Tupelo. While he is waiting in the Memphis train station, a number of children surround him as he sits reading the Jewish newspaper the *Forward*. The children stare at him and murmur to each other about his strange clothes and his large black top hat. Adults are looking at him as well. The Chabadnik, a sweet-tempered man possessed of a good sense of humor, smiles, eyes twinkling, and says to the children and the adults who are now all staring fixedly at him, "Whatsa matter? None of you never seen a Yankee?"

It is not difficult to see much beyond the surface of this joke, especially since the Chabadnik is from the commonwealth of Massachusetts. But underneath the funny surface is a broader meaning: that even the most foreign-looking American, a Jew who looks like a throwback to the Middle Ages, can claim to be a Yankee, especially if he resides in New England. Jews like the Chabadnik don't exactly trace their ancestry to the *Mayflower*—but as both U.S. citizens (Yanks) and Northerners, they can stand (or in this case sit) patriotic and proud. Yet a deeper meaning lies in the painful recognition of how Hasidim are often treated as strangers in a strange land in their own land. They often live apart from other Americans and, though citizens, continue, because of their alien-looking features and dress, to inspire curiosity, wonder, and xenophobia.

Chabadniks can feel utterly separate from secular and Reform Jews who, in turn, can and do feel utterly separate from Chabadniks and often view them as they might an alien species. All too many young Jews in California, where I live, or in many regions of the country other than the urban East, would not know a Chabadnik if they saw one ("Are those the Amish people?" a Jewish kid, seeing a bunch of Chabadniks, asks his parents).

Steve Stein goes back to his old neighborhood in Cleveland. He had served as a soldier in Vietnam and had not been back since. He is now a successful businessman and his travels take him to his roots. Everything has changed in the old neighborhood. Where Al's Kosher Butcher Shop used to be there now is a Korean grocery store; where Sam and Bernie's Dry Cleaning stood there is now a Burger King; and where Kaplan's Creamery was there is now a Gap. All has changed except for Kleinman's Shoe Repair, as poorly lit as ever and with the same narrow storefront, but still in business. Stein suddenly remembers that before he went to Vietnam, he left a pair of shoes with Mr. Kleinman that he never picked up. He wonders if they possibly could still be there.

He goes into the shop with its faint light and a small clanging bell rings.

Mr. Kleinman is bent across his work space in his leather apron with one eye nearly shut.

"Excuse me, Mr. Kleinman," Stein says. "I used to live around the corner, and forty years ago I left a pair of shoes with you for repair. Is it possible you still have them?"

Kleinman looks at Stein and says, "Vas dey black ving tips?"

Stein remembers and says, "Yes. They were!"

"And you vanted a half sole mit rubber heels?"

"Yes," says Stein. "That is exactly what I wanted."

"And you vanted taps on the heels only?"

"Yes!" says Stein. "Do you still have them?"

Mr. Kleinman looks up at him, squints, and says, "Dey be ready Vendsday."

Another sweet generational joke, this one points out how much things change in the New World, but also how much they stay the same, in the figure of the old shoemaker, a refugee and a vestige of the older shtetl world. The American Jew, now a businessman, goes back to the old neighborhood, once a kind of American shtetl, only to discover that all but the shoe repair place and the old shoemaker have vanished. What draws him back to the old neighborhood but memory? Only when he sees the old shoemaker's shop, the last trace of his childhood, does a memory of the shoes he left return. The old shoemaker remembers everything about the shoes and will not deviate from the task or his dedication to getting the job done. The significance of the joke is not only in the shoes still being there but the fact that the job will be done and the shoes will be ready for pickup. The two Jews, so different from each other in generation and financial success, are united in being Jews, and the joke teaches that Jews whose memories are still working are fated to remember.

Conclusion & Outtakes

When I began to write this book I not only wanted to include a lifetime's collection of Jewish jokes and stories, I also wanted to see if I could answer the question I had grappled with for years. Why are Jews funny?

I often think of much Jewish humor as being tied to the famous folk figure of the golem. The golem was the human-created power, like the monster in Mary Shelley's *Franken-stein*, fashioned to defend the ghetto of Prague from pogroms and violent anti-Semitism, to be both defensive and combative.

This book is by no means exhaustive. There is much I did not include. But let me add just a few more jokes that I still prize—like the outtakes or bits that follow a good, funny movie. I want to keep with the spirit of the book, which is to keep the jokes coming. For instance, the silly chauvinistic joke about how the Jews obviously invented air-conditioning. The names you see on every unit: Lo, Norm, Hi, and Max.

Or the Jewish American princess line, delivered unwittingly, by a young Jewish woman to my niece Susan on a Birthright trip. The purpose of the all-expense-paid trip to Israel for Jewish youth is to instill a love for the Jewish homeland, perhaps even to inspire youth to make *aliyah*—a return from the Diaspora to live in the Jewish state. As the two traveled along with a busful of other young Jews, the young woman suddenly turned to my niece and said, out of the blue, "I would consider making *aliyah*, but the shopping here sucks."

I continue to relish the gifted Canadian Jewish author Mordecai Richler's true tale of a band of Jewish boys turning anti-Semitism on its head by stealing a sign on a Montreal beach that read NO JEWS ALLOWED, and then putting it back after crossing out "Jews" and writing "Litvaks," the word for Lithuanian Jews that is also used for the Orthodox. Or, the brilliant comic bit of Woody Allen's in which he plays the proverbial schlemiel shooting a moose; upon realizing it is not dead, he takes the moose with him to a costume party, where it gets furious after losing best costume prize to a couple named Berkowitz who are at the party dressed as a moose.

I have more encounters with great comics to invoke. Jokes often change and mutate, I remember telling the comedian

Alan King before an interview the two of us did onstage. I had heard another version of his great line about the man who opens a Chinese fortune cookie and finds the message "Help! I'm a prisoner inside a Chinese fortune cookie factory." In the version I heard, the message was inside a mezuzah and said "Help! I'm being held prisoner in a mezuzah factory."

A quick non sequitur silly joke. I obviously can't help myself. Alan King once performed at Buckingham Palace and was greeted by Queen Elizabeth and Prince Philip after the show. The queen welcomed him by saying, "How do you do, Mr. King," and King said, "How do you do, Mrs. Queen."

I offered, by the way, to have a joke-off with King onstage. He declined, saying he tells stories not jokes.

I, obviously, prefer both.

Would that there were world and time enough to include many others since many other Jewish jokes continue to hold up through the years. Like the one in which a Jew is standing in the middle of the Warsaw train station with several suitcases. He needs to use the bathroom so he asks a passerby:

"Excuse me, sir, are you an anti-Semite?"

"No, of course not!" the man replies. "I am actually quite fond of Jews."

The Jew thanks him and asks the next passerby, "Excuse me, sir, are you an anti-Semite?"

"Absolutely not! We love the Jews! We hid Jews at our house during the war!"

The Jew thanks him and asks the same question to the next passerby: "Excuse me, sir, are you an anti-Semite?"

"I most certainly am! I hate the filthy Jews! Our country would be better off without them!"

"At last, an honest man!" says the Jew. "Would you mind watching my bags while I go to the bathroom?"

I have tried to explain thematic meaning in the great Jewish jokes, but what of humor from Jews that defies explanation in terms of any Jewish theme? Humor from Jewish comics that brings laughter simply because the joke or the bit is funny? Was Andy Kaufman's weird and offbeat brand of humor tied in any way to his being Jewish? What of other comics who happen to be Jewish but have created their own original brands? Such as Paul Reubens (a.k.a. Pee-wee Herman) or Gilbert Gottfried? Or what of the satiric humor of the raunchy, oversexed, brilliant Howard Stern. The self-proclaimed king of all media is, in reality, the king of Jewish bad boys who sprinkles his shtick with Yiddish. Stern assumed the role on his radio show, not too long ago, of an Indian-accented (therefore outsourced) adviser answering phone calls on "the ISIS Hotline." He fielded questions. Like one about the best way to behead a Jew.

Humor out of suffering? Dark humor? Yes. But Stern's

humor, except when he is tearing himself down or ridiculing others, is often difficult to pigeonhole. There is, however, the Jewish lineage—what he calls the major humor influence of his youth—the Jewish guys who gave us *Mad* magazine.

Hard to classify, I would add, is the madcap humor of Sacha Baron Cohen. He managed, as his character Bruno, to fool a former Mossad agent and a Palestinian academic into at least initially believing he was questioning them seriously in Jerusalem about the connection between Hamas and hummus.

In these pages, there is a tremendous and often hilarious range of tribal humor. The Jewish jokes, stories, and anecdotes, I hope, have brought and will continue to bring laughter. They should also bring deep appreciation for the remarkably wide-ranging genius of Jewish comedy. Like Jewish food, the jokes and humor feed memory, emotion, nostalgia, identity, community, and longing. Perhaps, as important, they can bring wisdom and meaning. The world will continue to change, often in ways that challenge, plague, and haunt us. But my hope is that the jokes and the humor will remain an ongoing part of many lives for, well, at least the next few thousand years.

Acknowledgments

I want to thank the friends who helped with suggestions or gave thoughtful responses or advice. Thanks to Rita Abrams, Rita Gershengorn, Jerry Jurinsky, Harlan Kleiman, Nikki Meredith, Gerry Nachman, Owen Renick, Judy Rich, Howard Schatz, David Spiegel, Loretta Stec, Manfred Wolf, and Dan Zoll. My gratitude to the great HarperCollins team of Alieza Schvimer, Amy Bendell, Lisa Sharkey, Emily Homonoff, Molly Waxman, Ryan Cury, Stephanie Vallejo, Mumtaz Mustafa, Bonni Leon-Berman, Sharyn Rosenblum and to my inimitable agent, Amy Rennert. Finally—special bountiful thanks to my wife and kids for their support and inspiration.